Beak & Ally

Snow Birds

Norm Feuti

HARPER alley

An Imprint of HarperCollinsPublishers

For Jen.

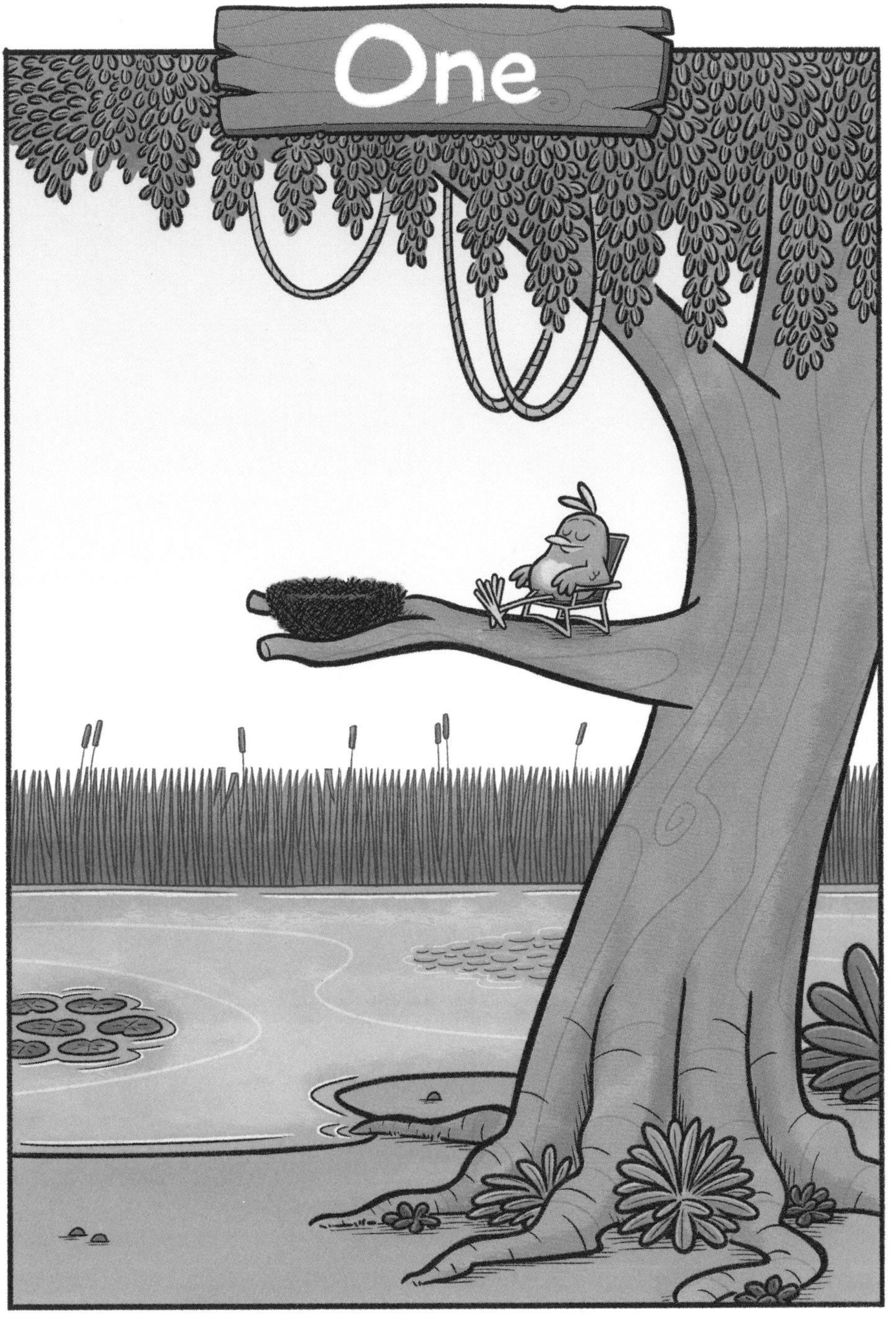
One

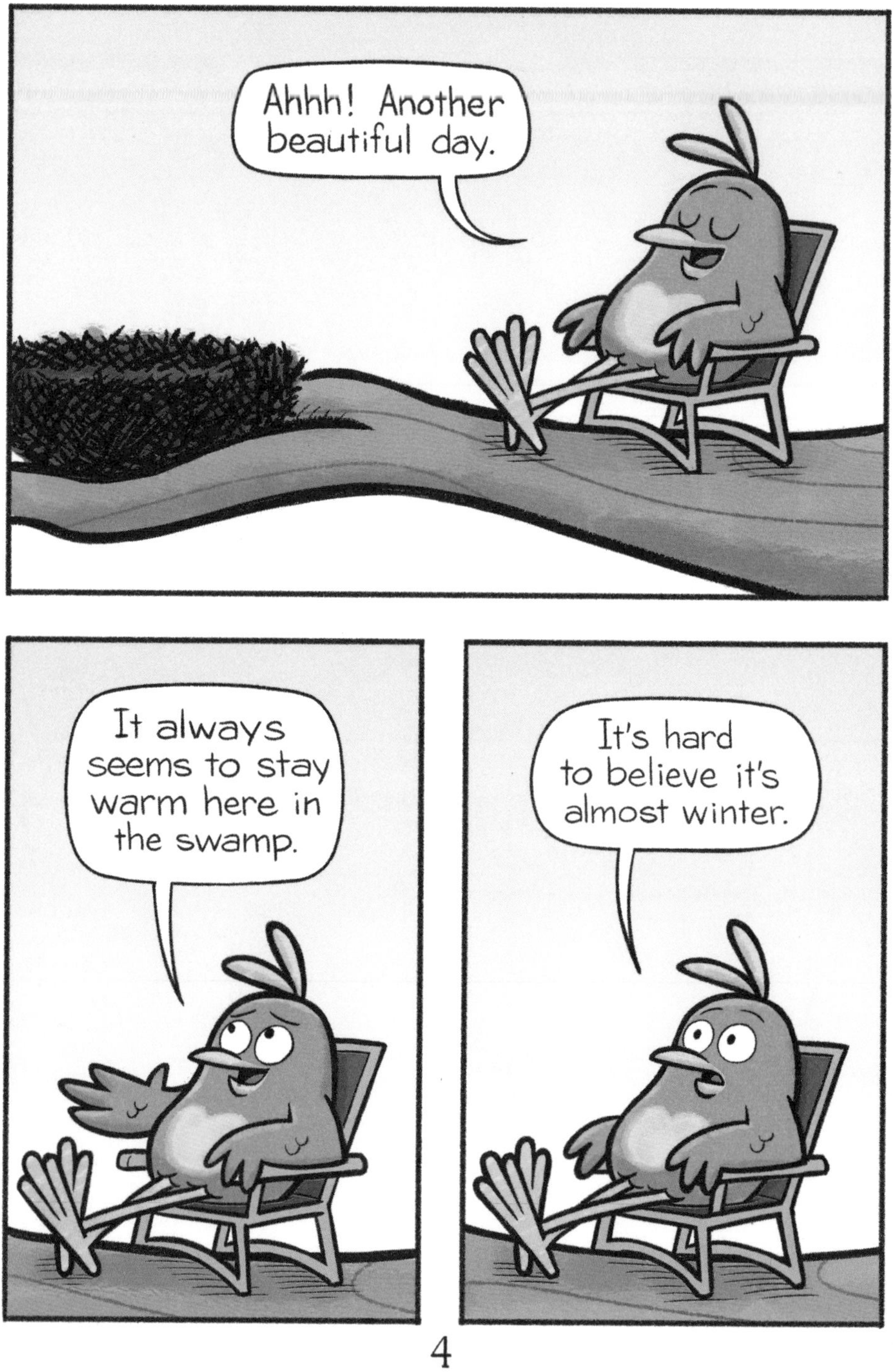
Ahhh! Another beautiful day.
It always seems to stay warm here in the swamp.
It's hard to believe it's almost winter.

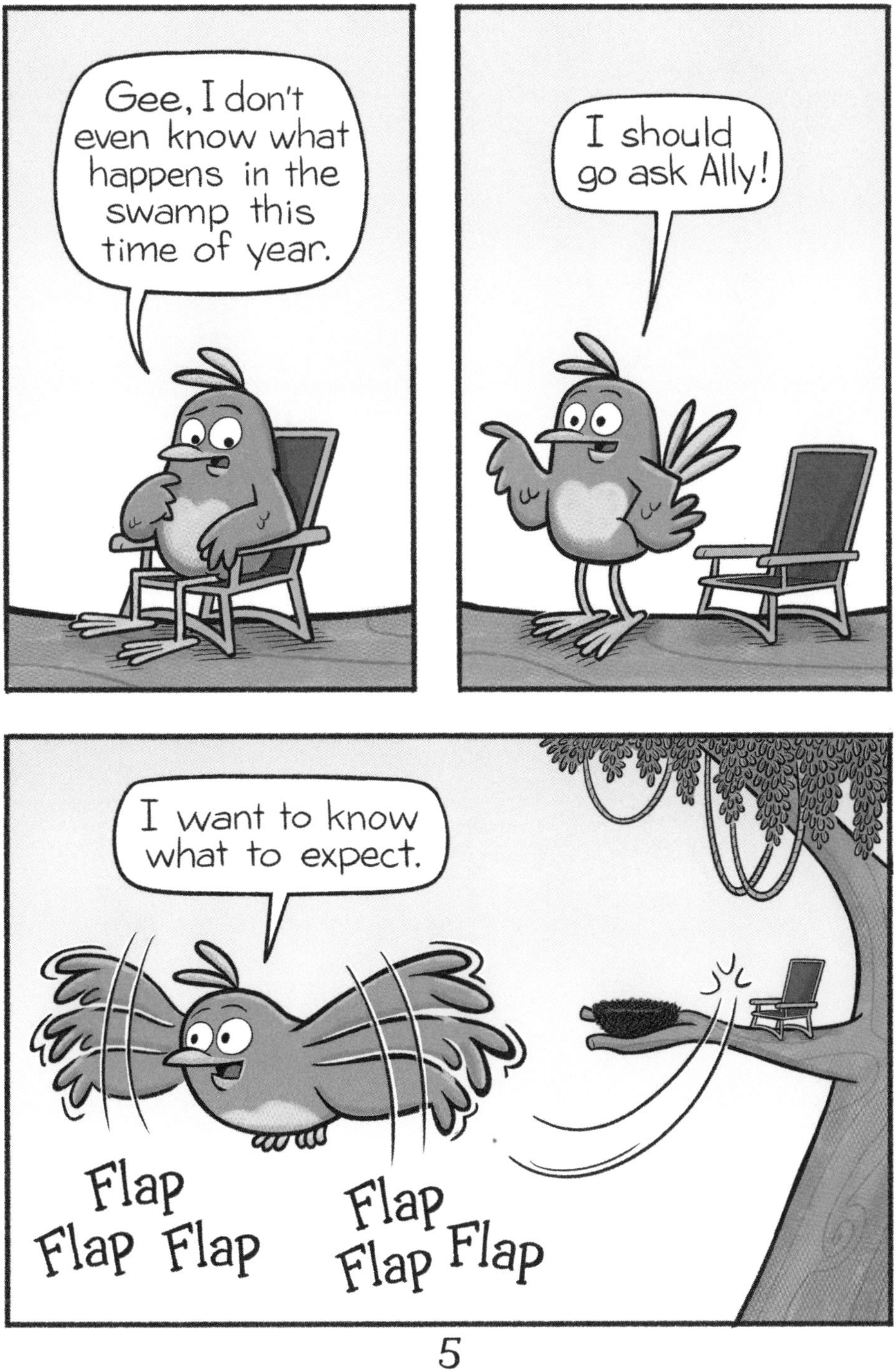
Gee, I don't even know what happens in the swamp this time of year.
I should go ask Ally!
I want to know what to expect.
Flap Flap Flap
Flap Flap Flap

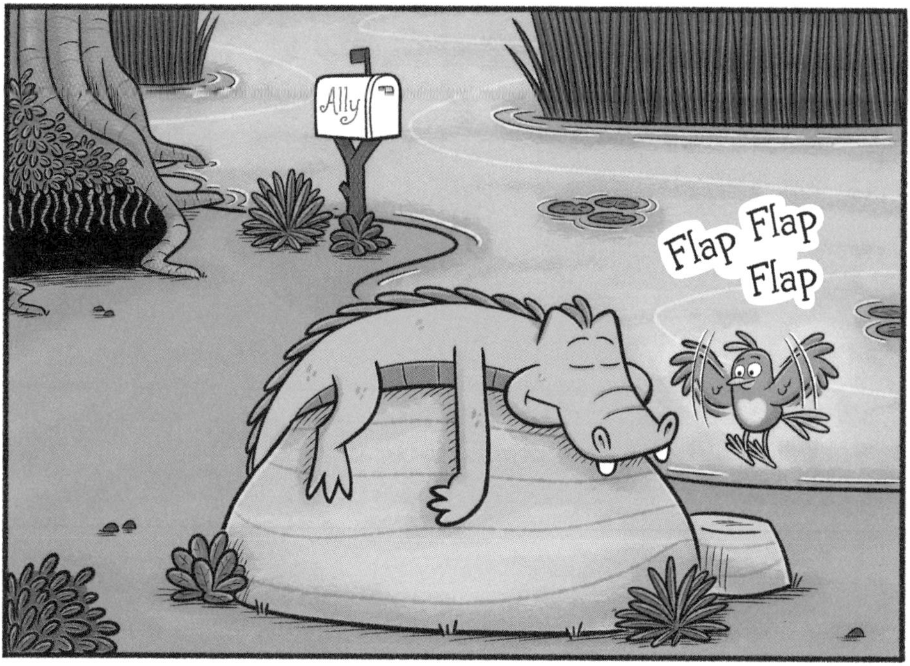
Ally
Flap Flap Flap

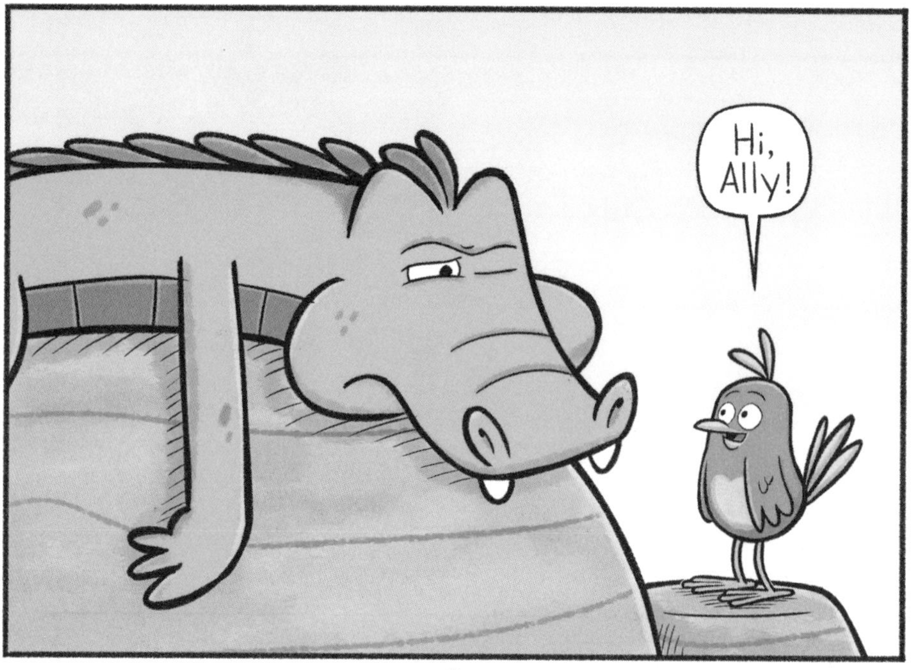
Hi, Ally!

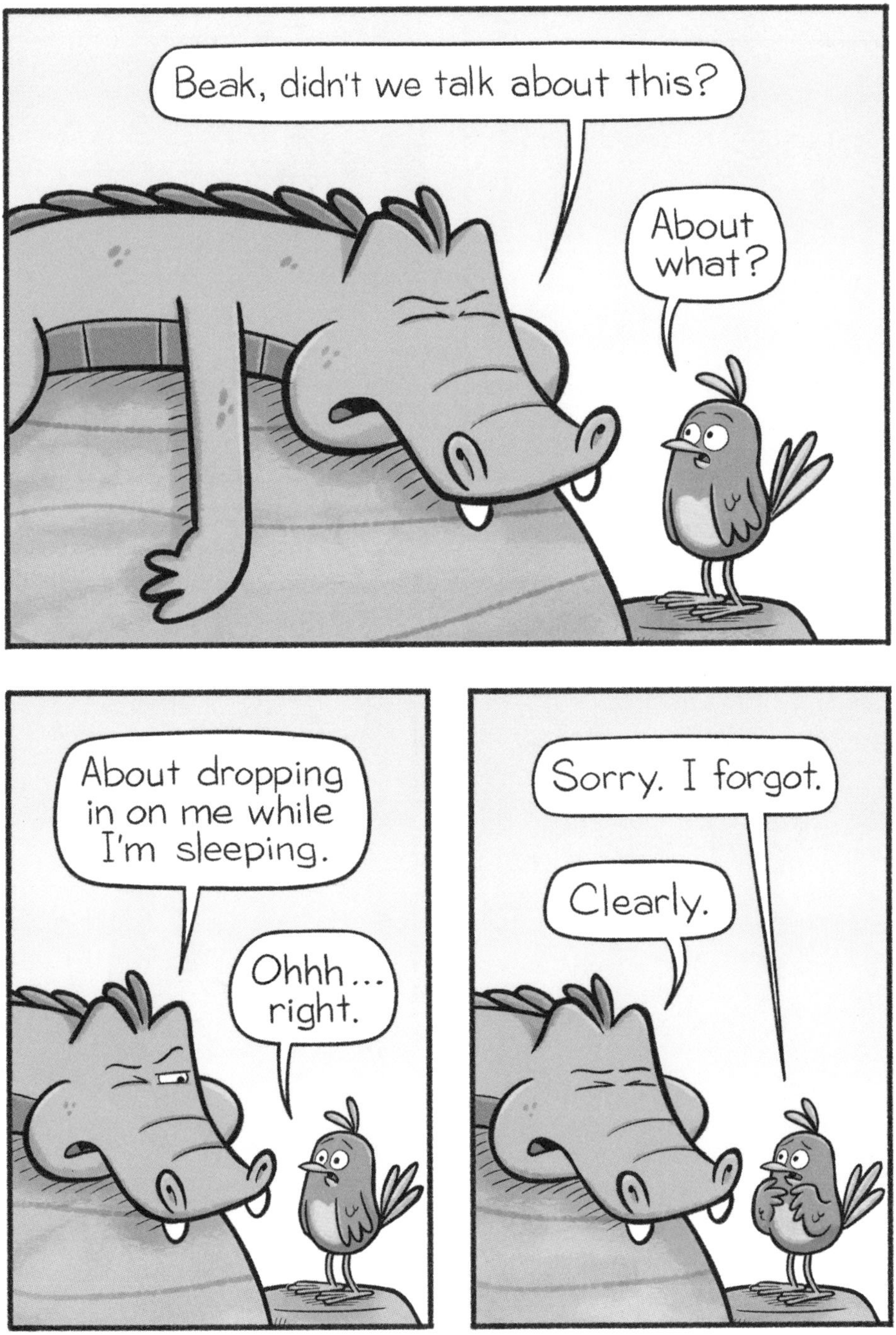
Beak, didn't we talk about this?
About what?
About dropping in on me while I'm sleeping.
Ohhh... right.
Sorry. I forgot.
Clearly.

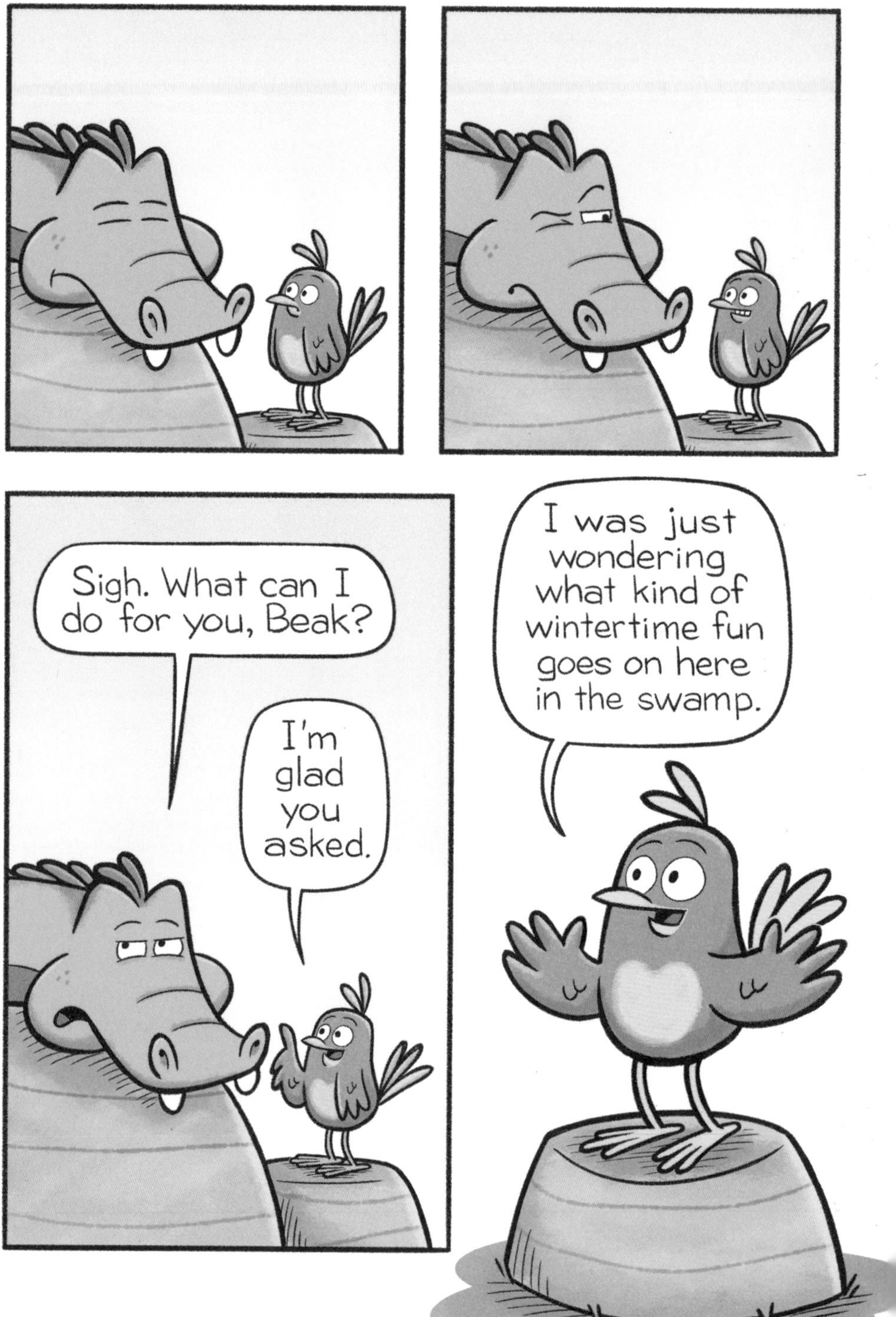
Sigh. What can I do for you, Beak?
I'm glad you asked.
I was just wondering what kind of wintertime fun goes on here in the swamp.

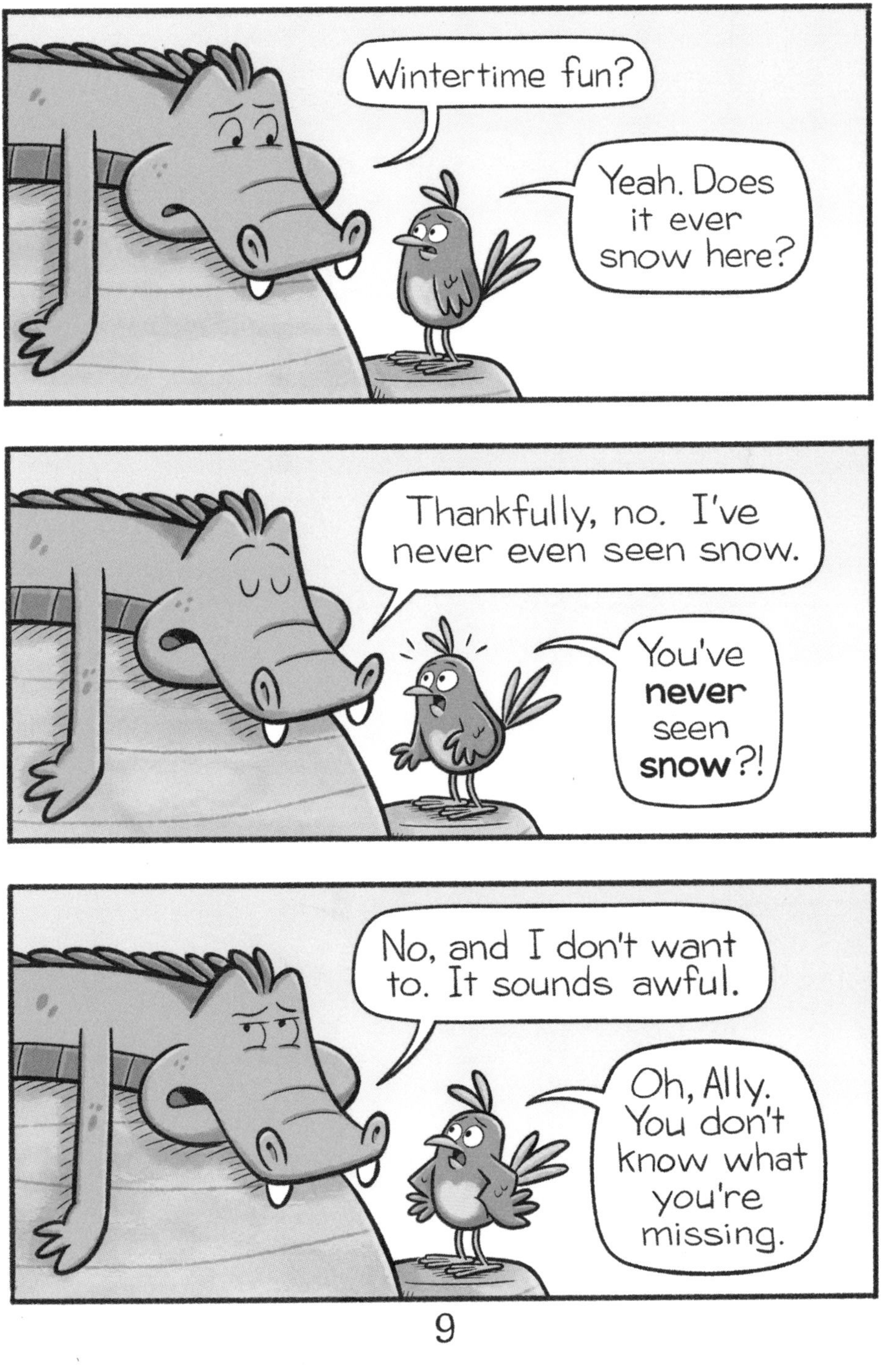
Wintertime fun?
Yeah. Does it ever snow here?
Thankfully, no. I've never even seen snow.
You've **never** seen **snow**?!
No, and I don't want to. It sounds awful.
Oh, Ally. You don't know what you're missing.

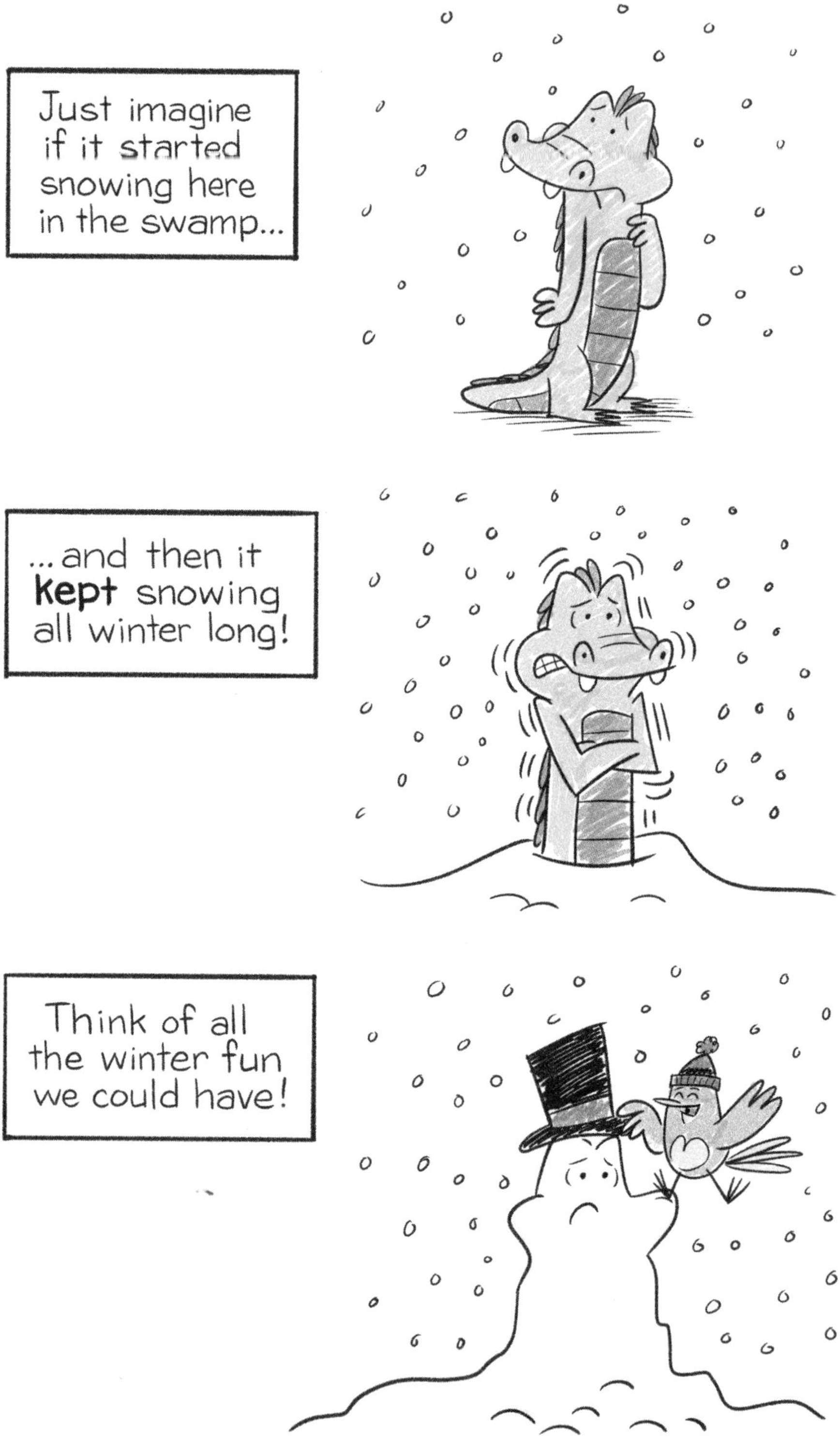
Just imagine if it started snowing here in the swamp...
...and then it **kept** snowing all winter long!
Think of all the winter fun we could have!

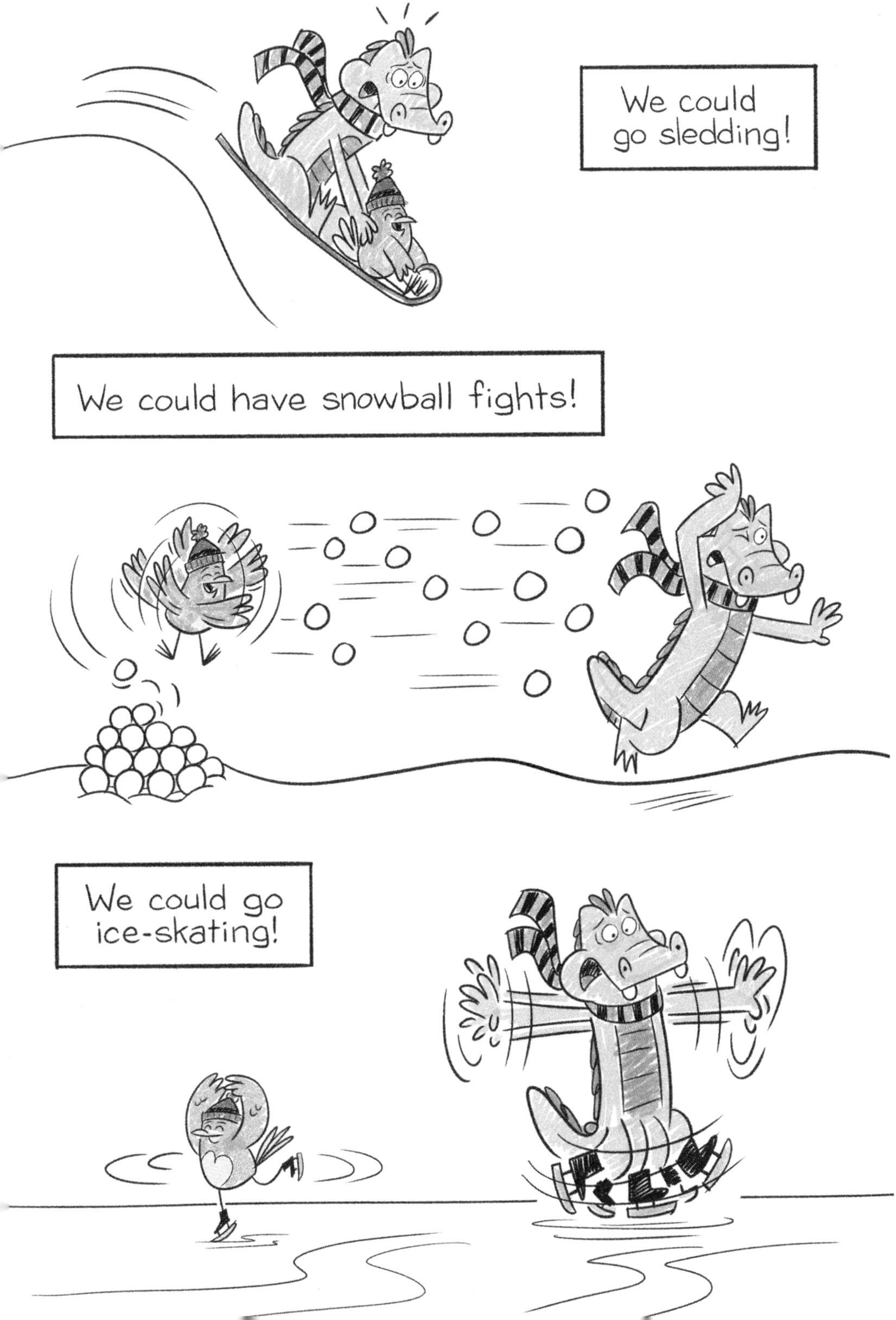
We could go sledding!
We could have snowball fights!
We could go ice-skating!

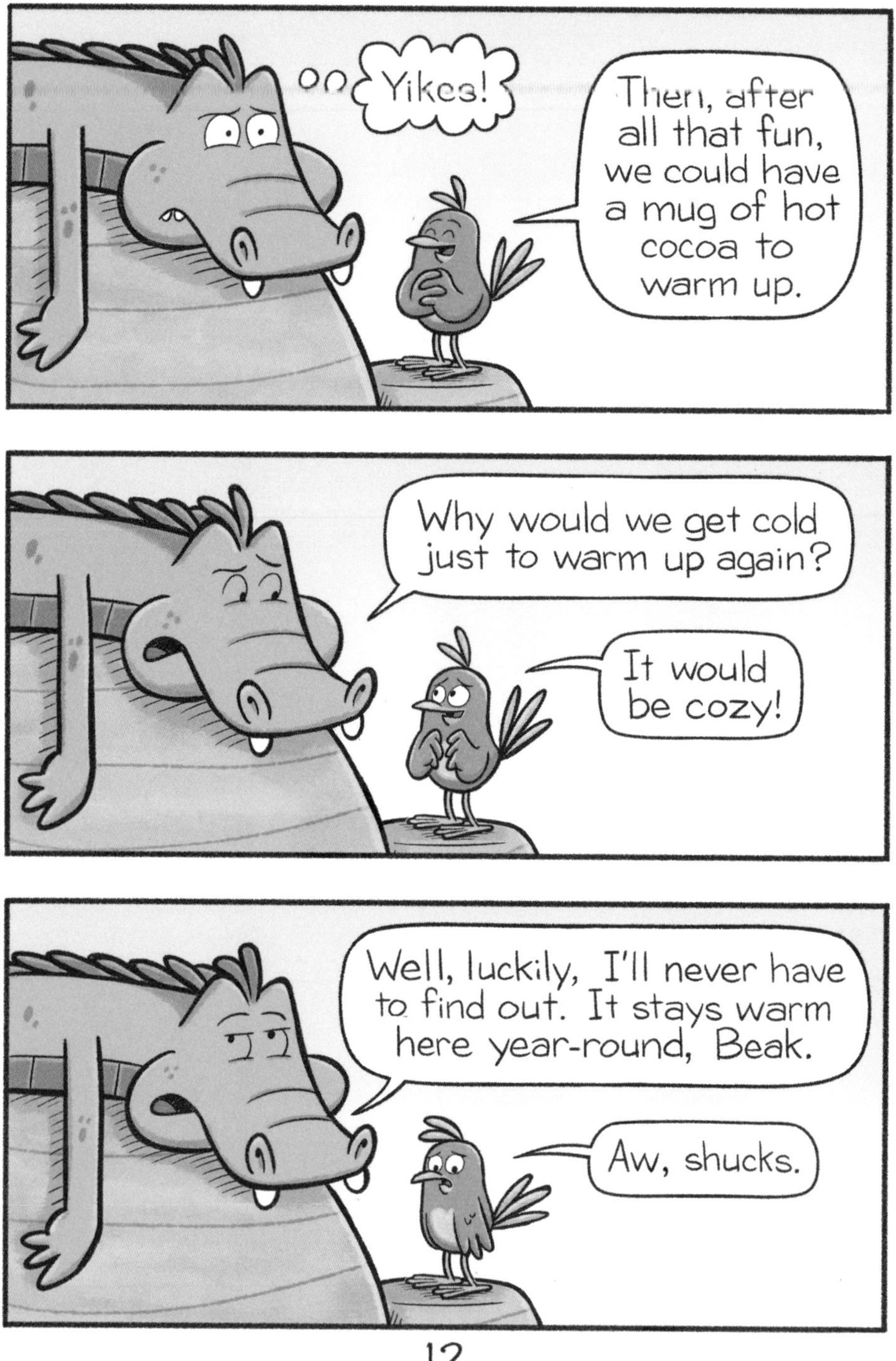
Yikes!
Then, after all that fun, we could have a mug of hot cocoa to warm up.
Why would we get cold just to warm up again?
It would be cozy!
Well, luckily, I'll never have to find out. It stays warm here year-round, Beak.
Aw, shucks.

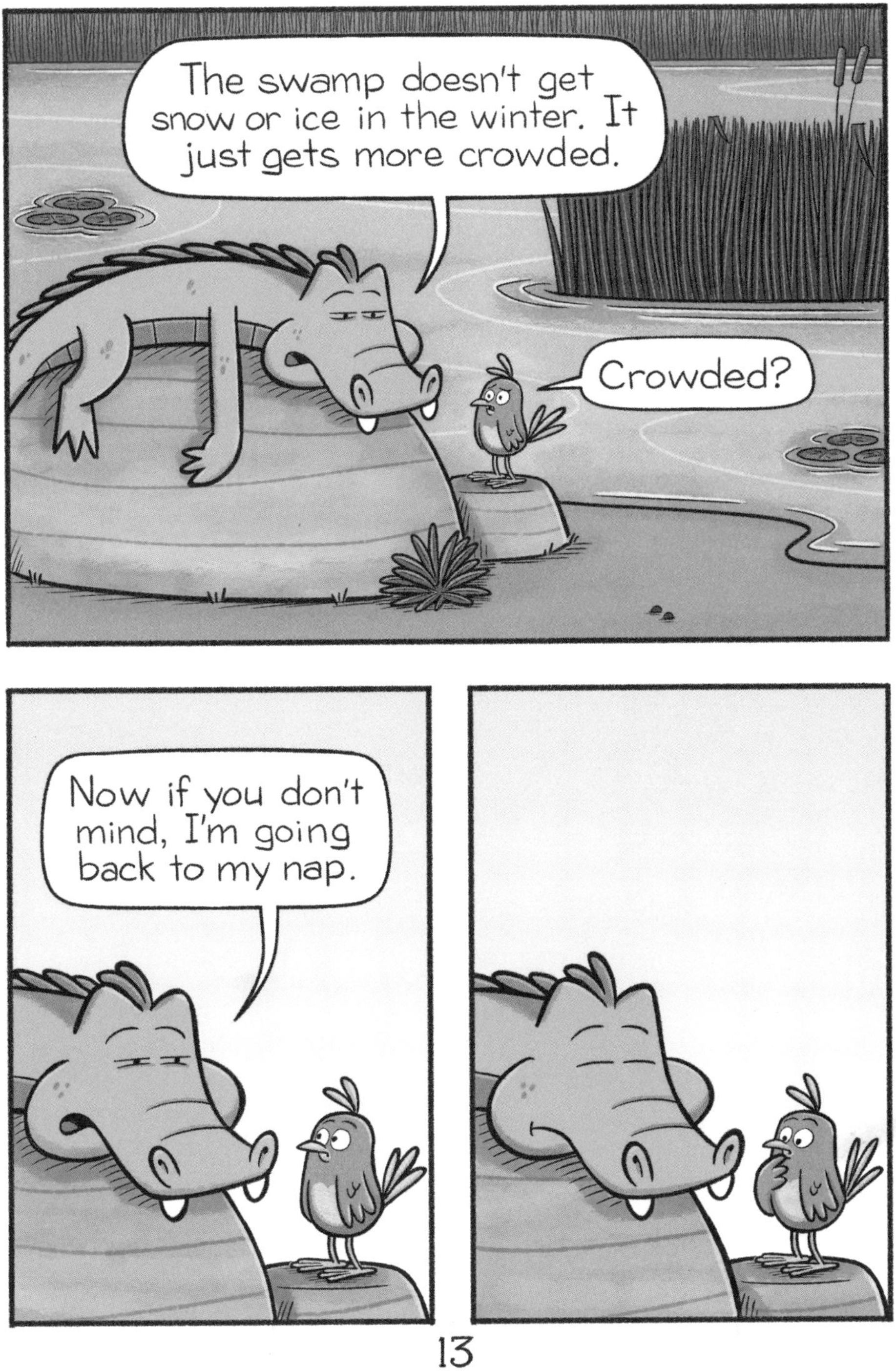
The swamp doesn't get snow or ice in the winter. It just gets more crowded.
Crowded?
Now if you don't mind, I'm going back to my nap.

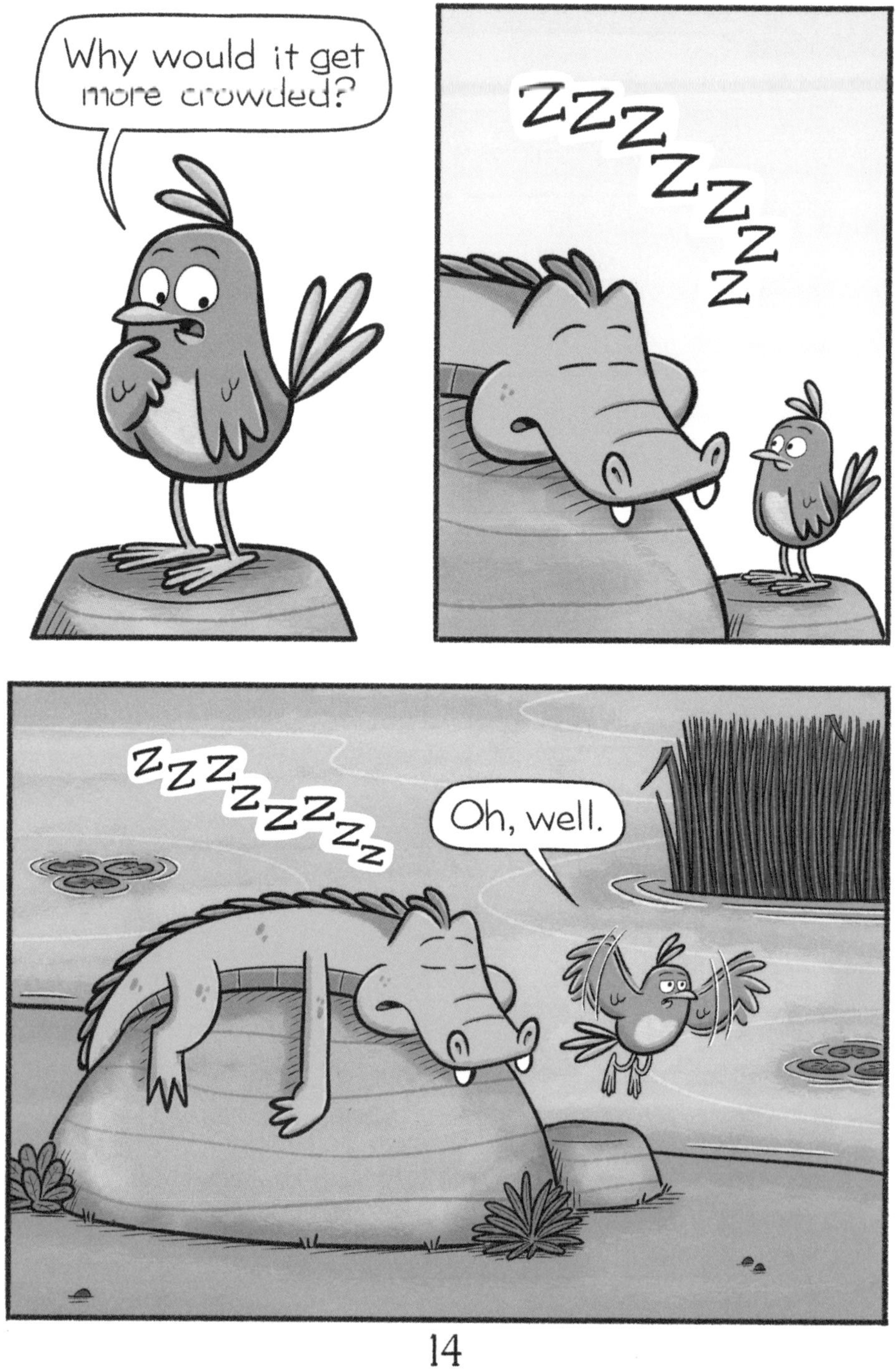
Why would it get more crowded?
ZZZZZZZZ
ZZZZZZZZZ
Oh, well.

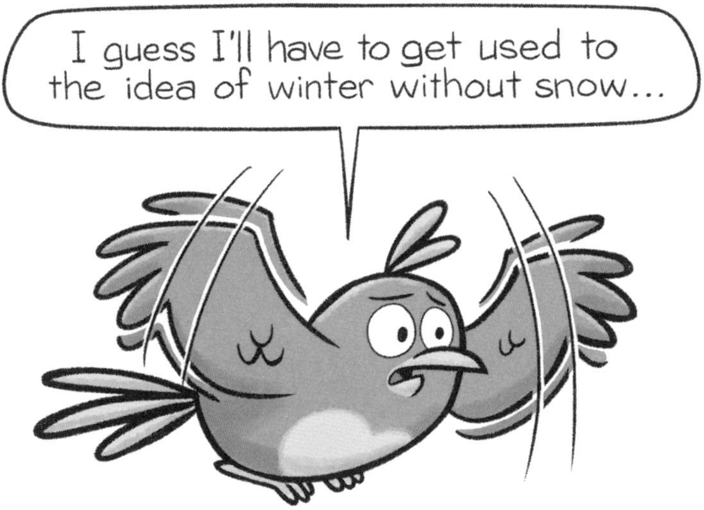
I guess I'll have to get used to the idea of winter without snow...

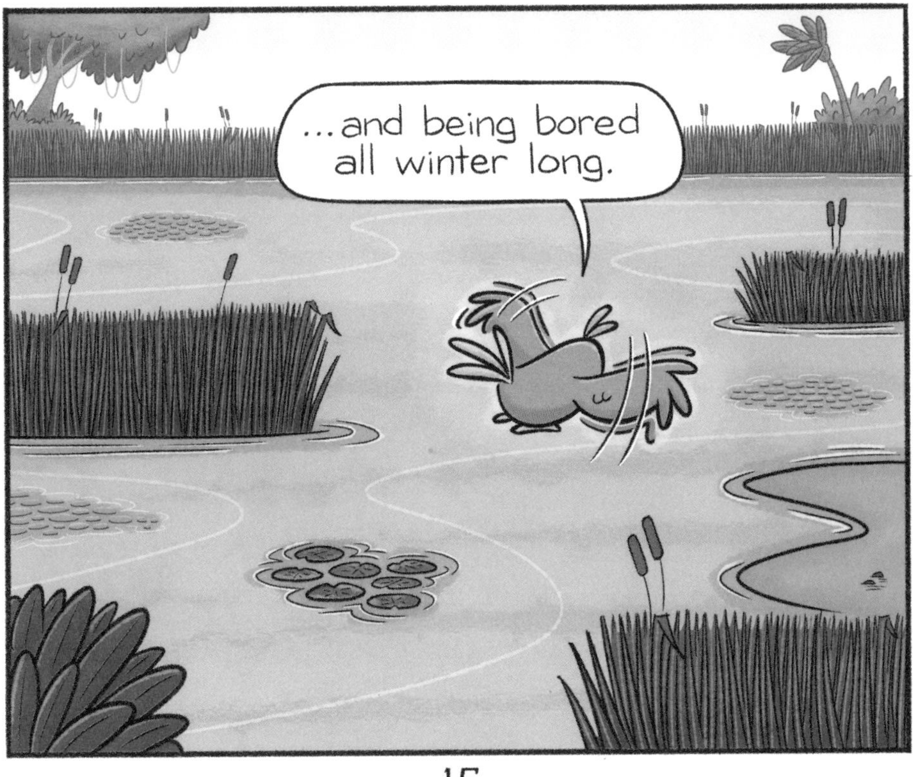
...and being bored all winter long.

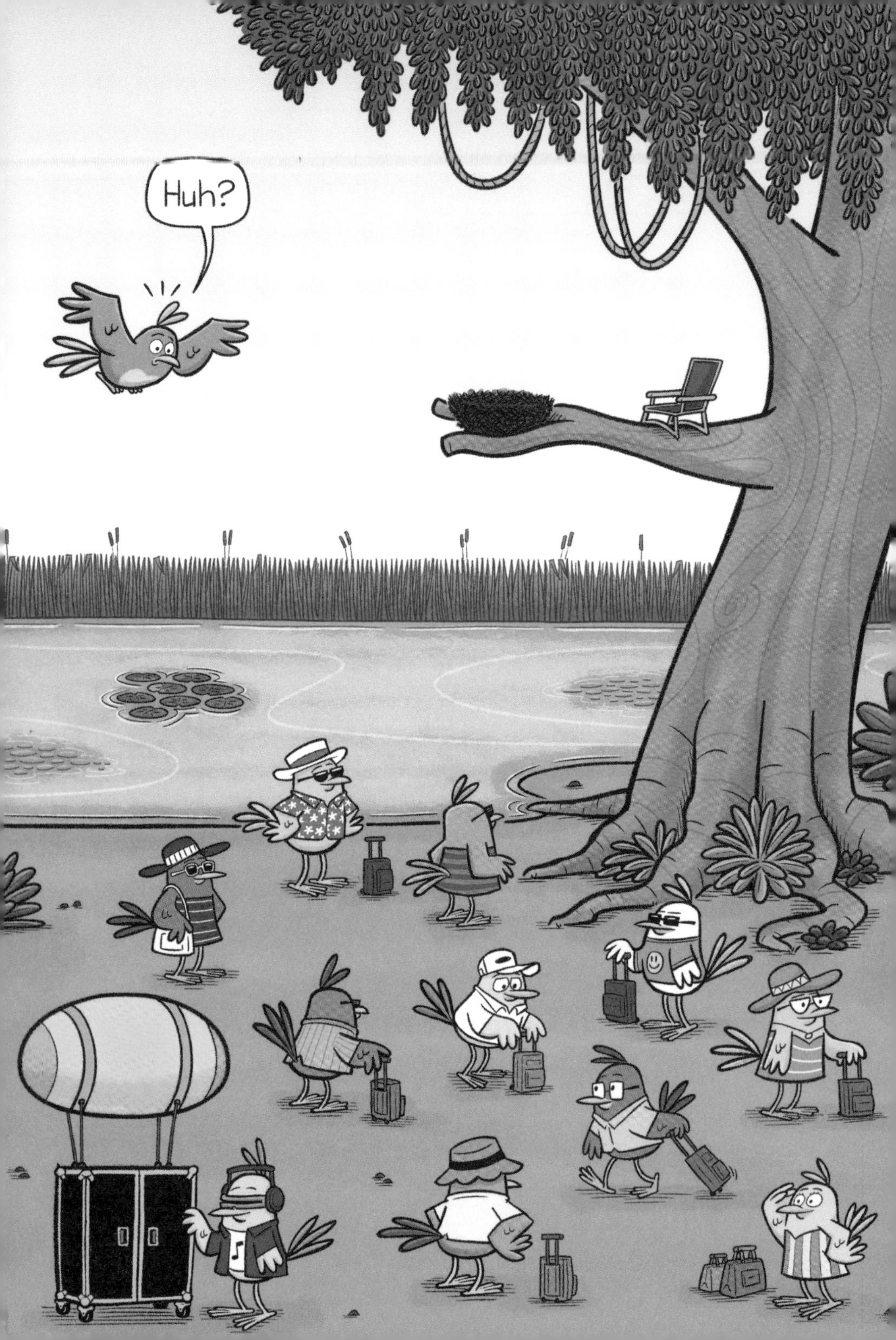
Huh?

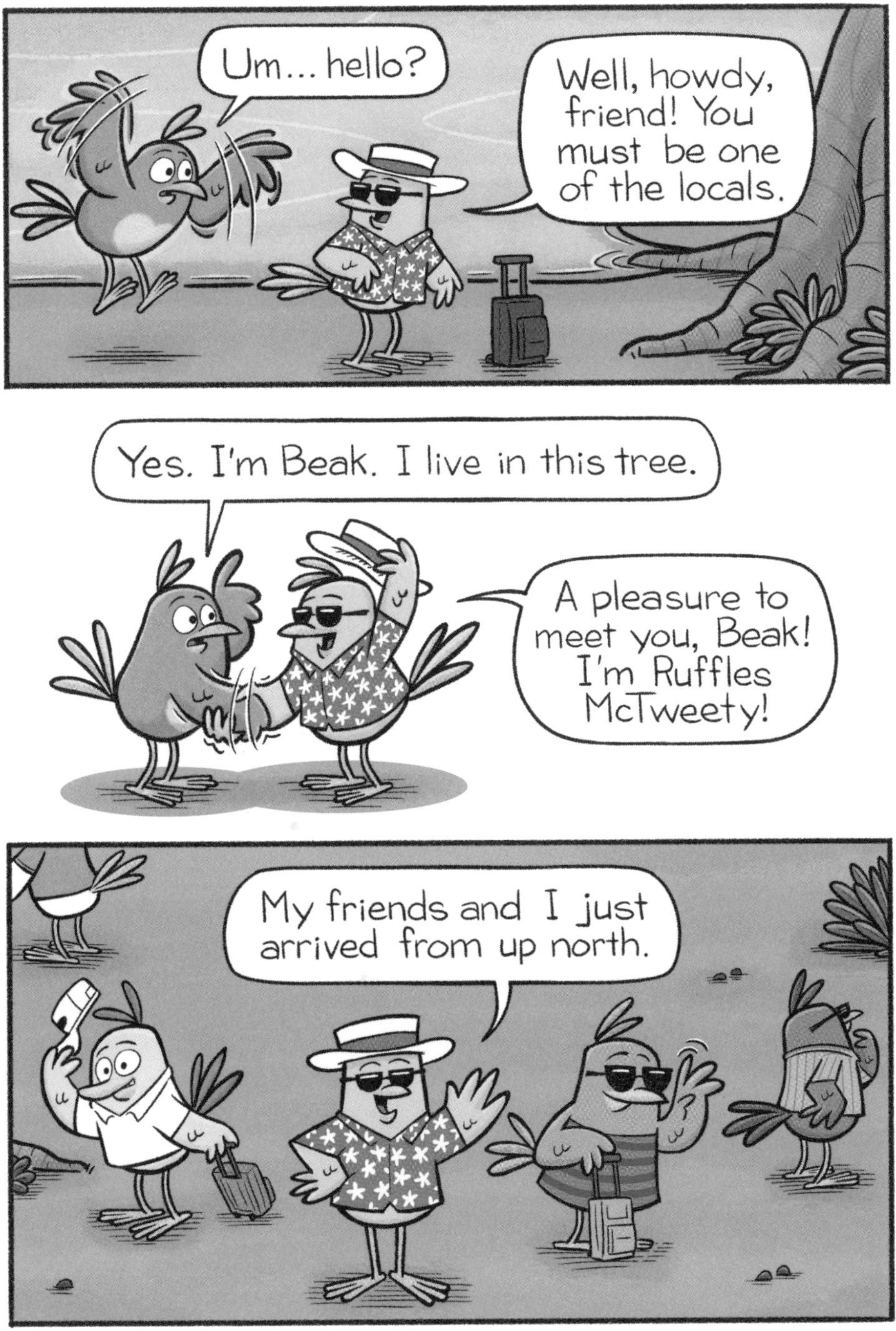
Um... hello?
Well, howdy, friend! You must be one of the locals.
Yes. I'm Beak. I live in this tree.
A pleasure to meet you, Beak! I'm Ruffles McTweety!
My friends and I just arrived from up north.

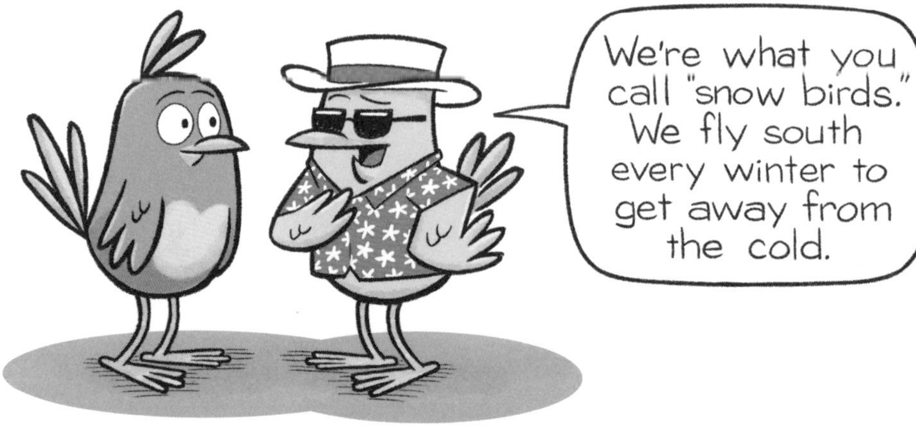
We're what you call "snow birds." We fly south every winter to get away from the cold.

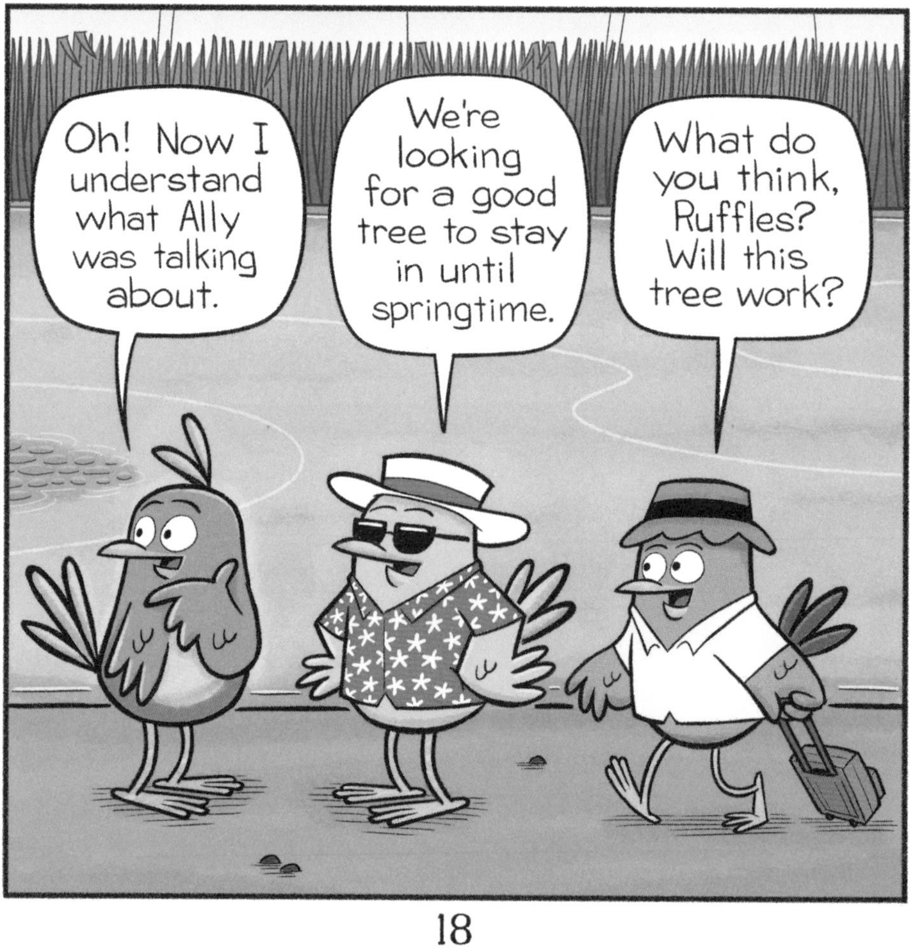
Oh! Now I understand what Ally was talking about.
We're looking for a good tree to stay in until springtime.
What do you think, Ruffles? Will this tree work?

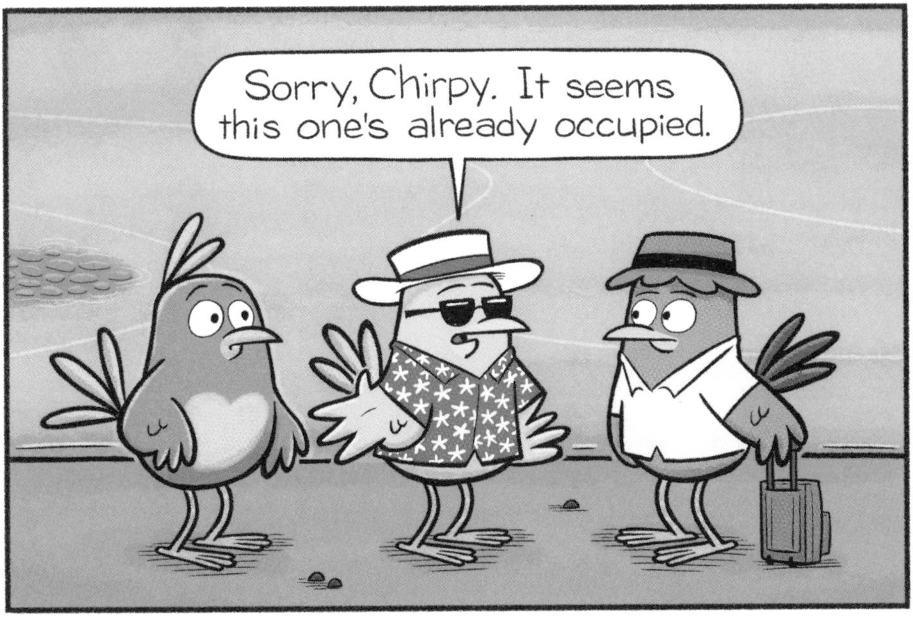
Sorry, Chirpy. It seems this one's already occupied.

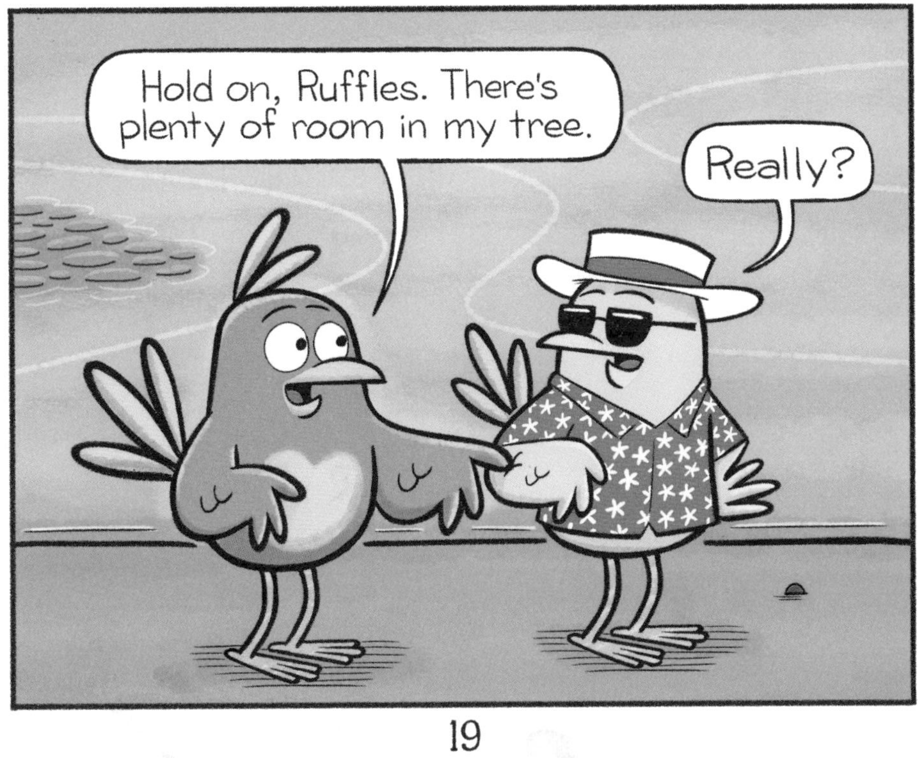
Hold on, Ruffles. There's plenty of room in my tree.
Really?

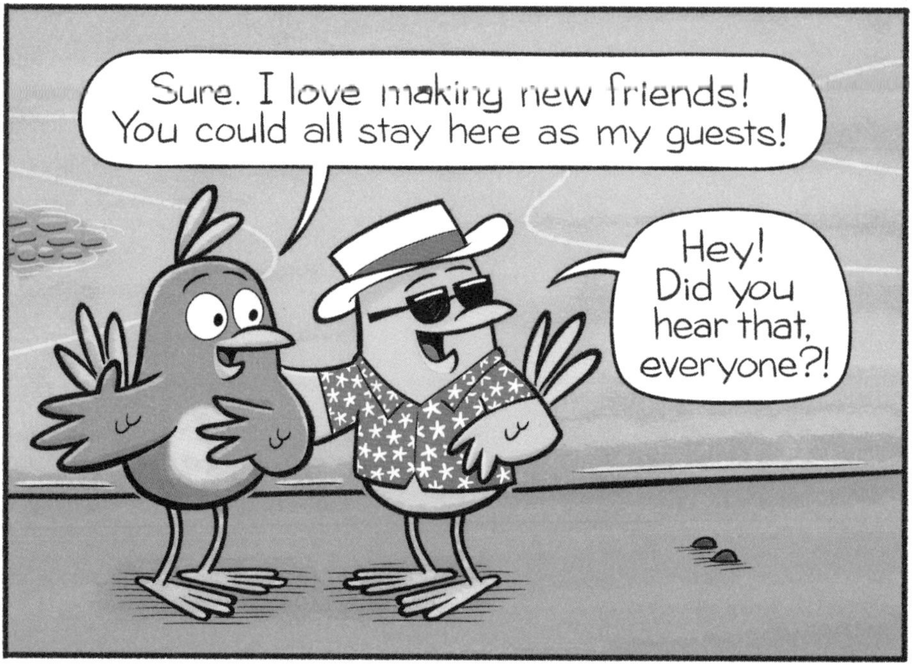
Sure. I love making new friends! You could all stay here as my guests!
Hey! Did you hear that, everyone?!

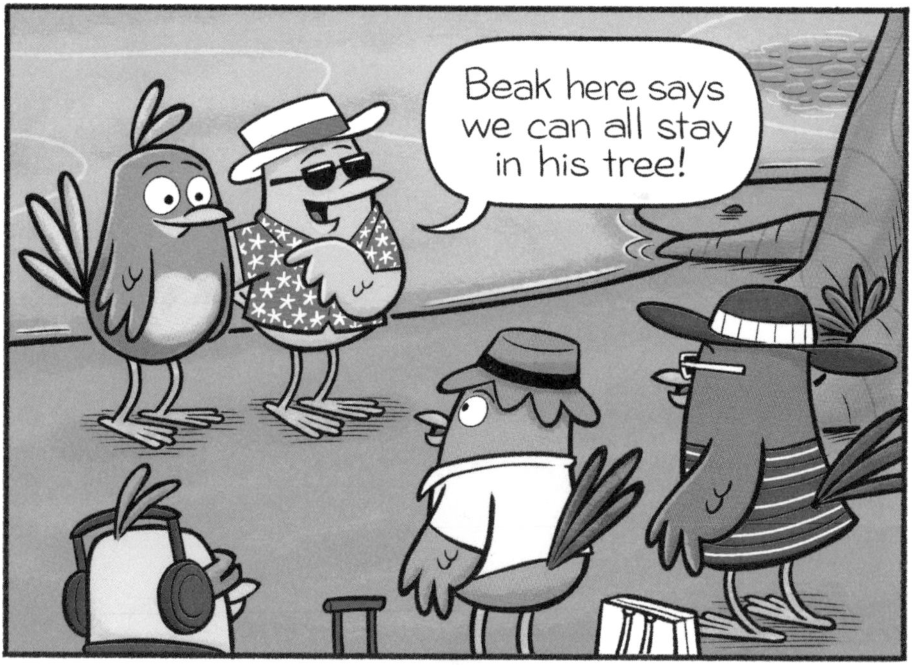
Beak here says we can all stay in his tree!

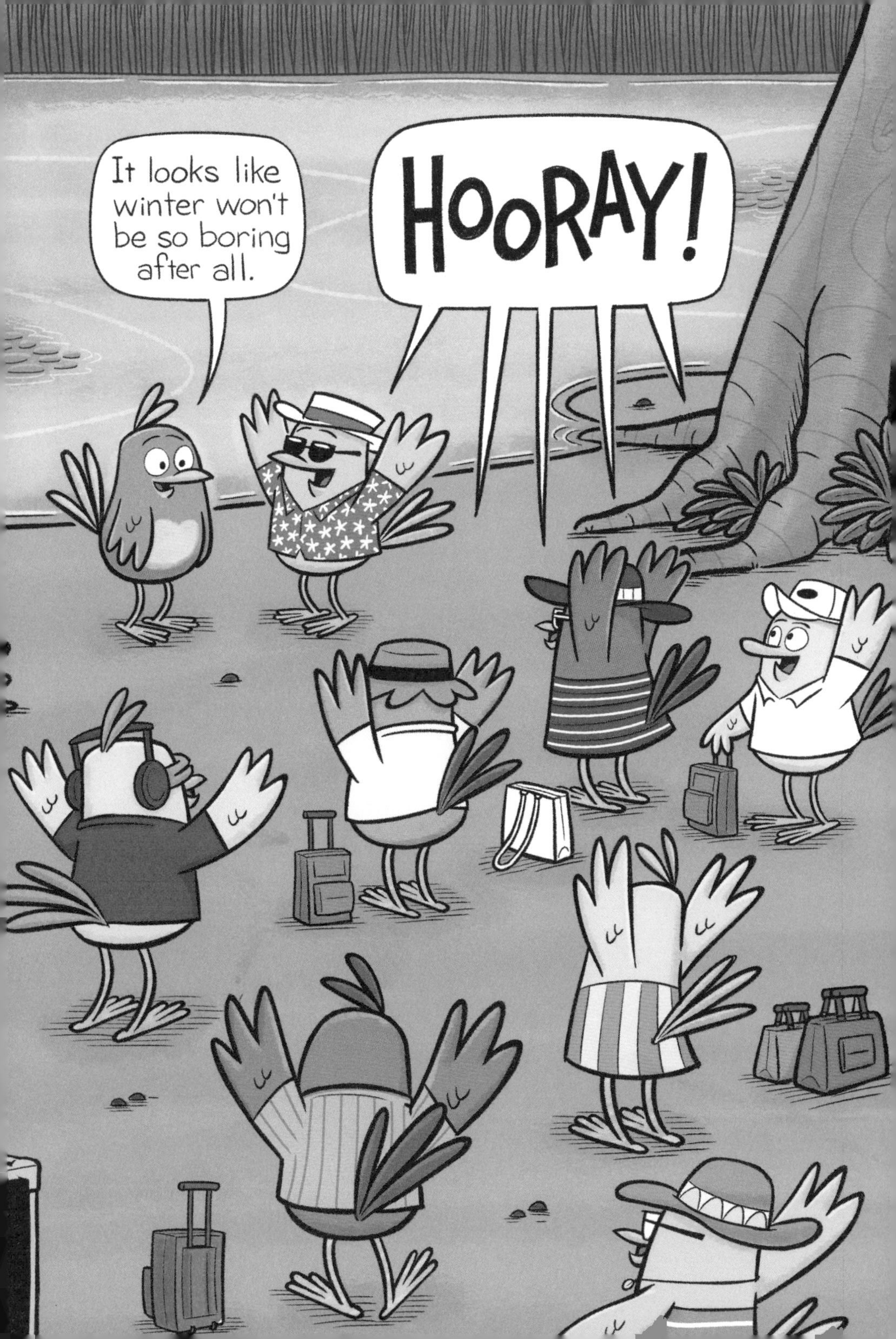
It looks like winter won't be so boring after all.
HOORAY!

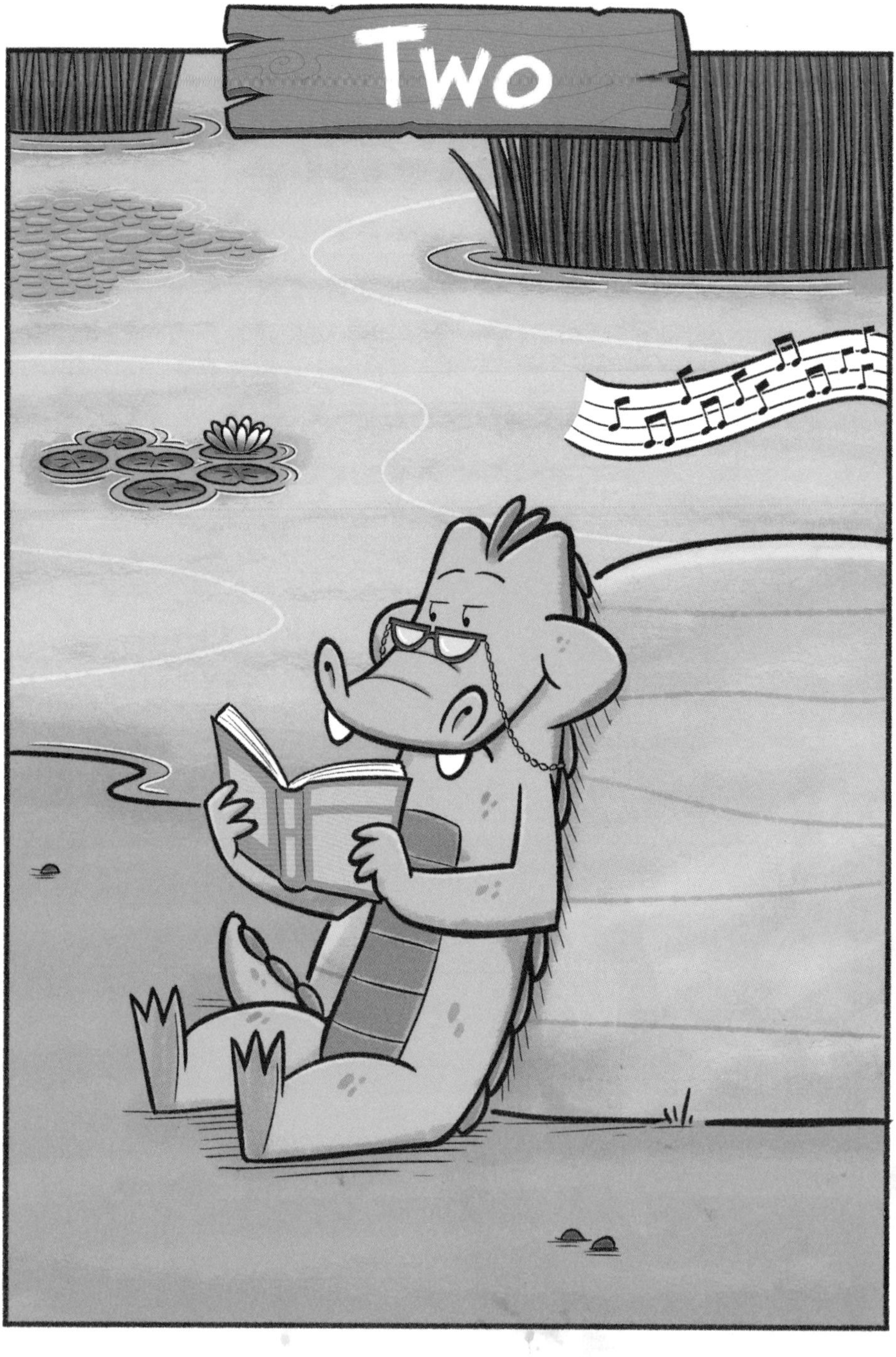
Two

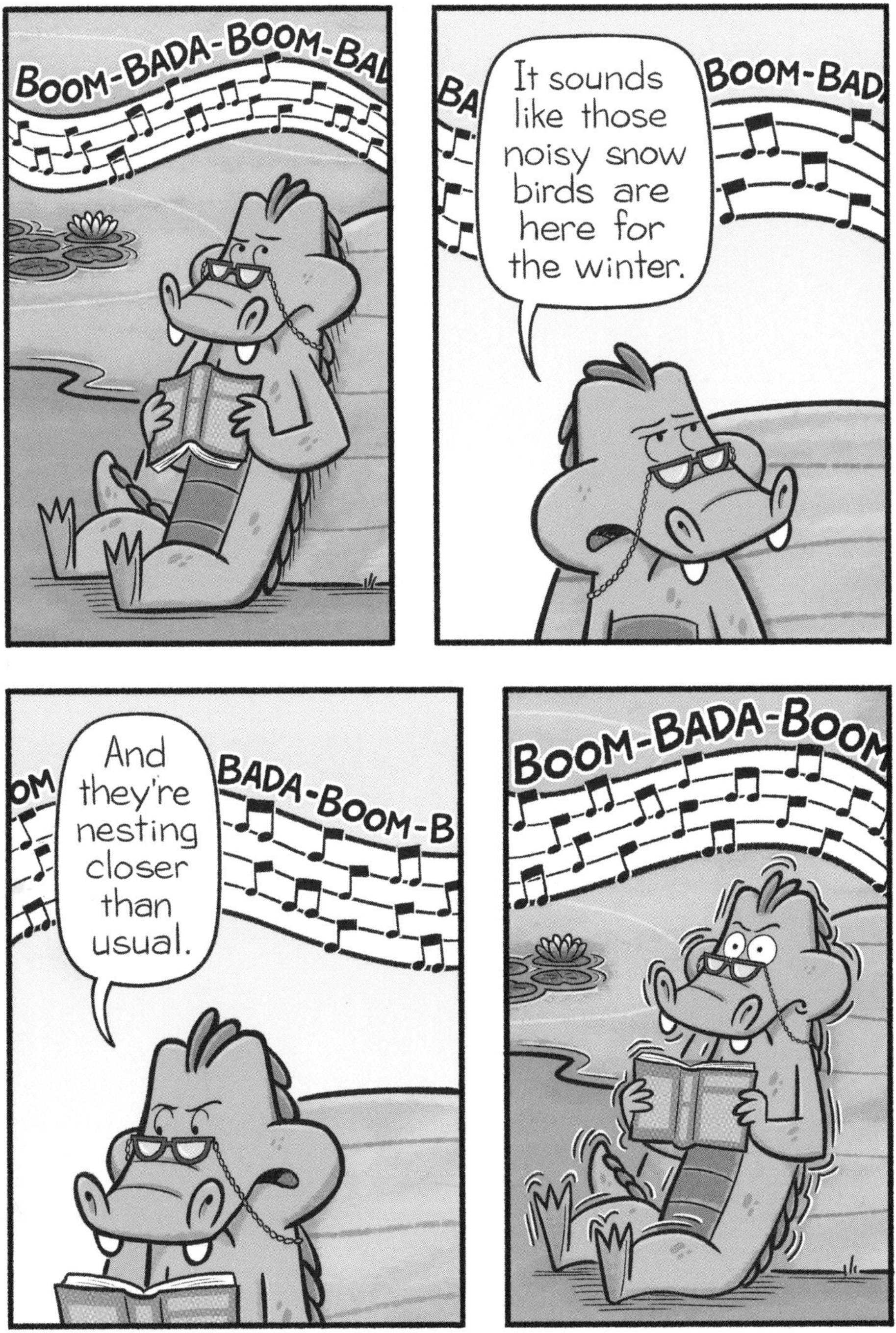
BOOM-BADA-BOOM-BAD
BA
It sounds like those noisy snow birds are here for the winter.
BOOM-BAD
OM
And they're nesting closer than usual.
BADA-BOOM-B
BOOM-BADA-BOOM

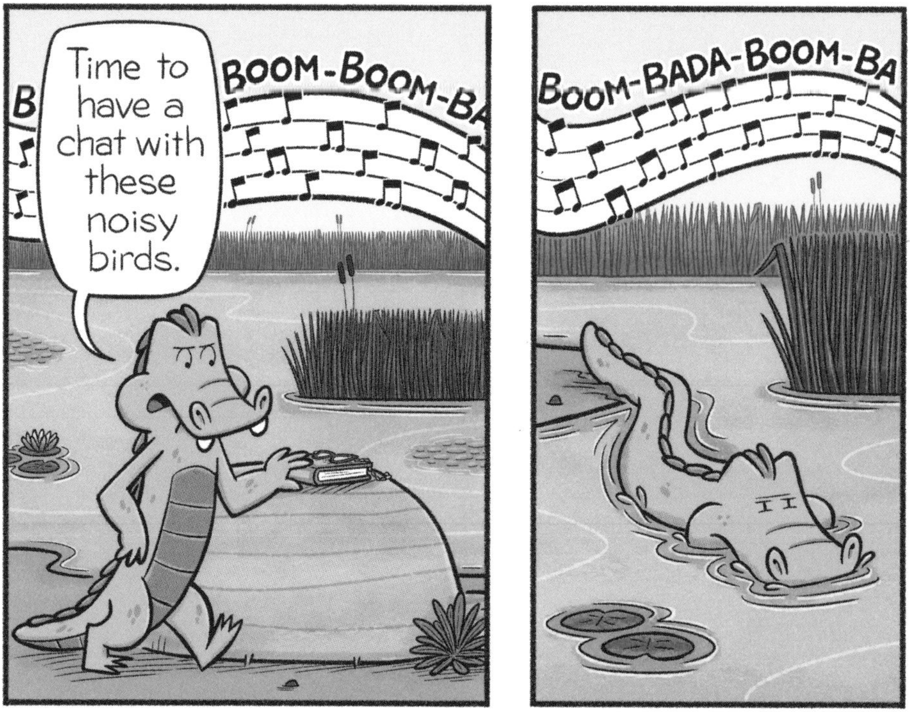
Time to have a chat with these noisy birds.
BOOM-BOOM-BA
BOOM-BADA-BOOM-BA

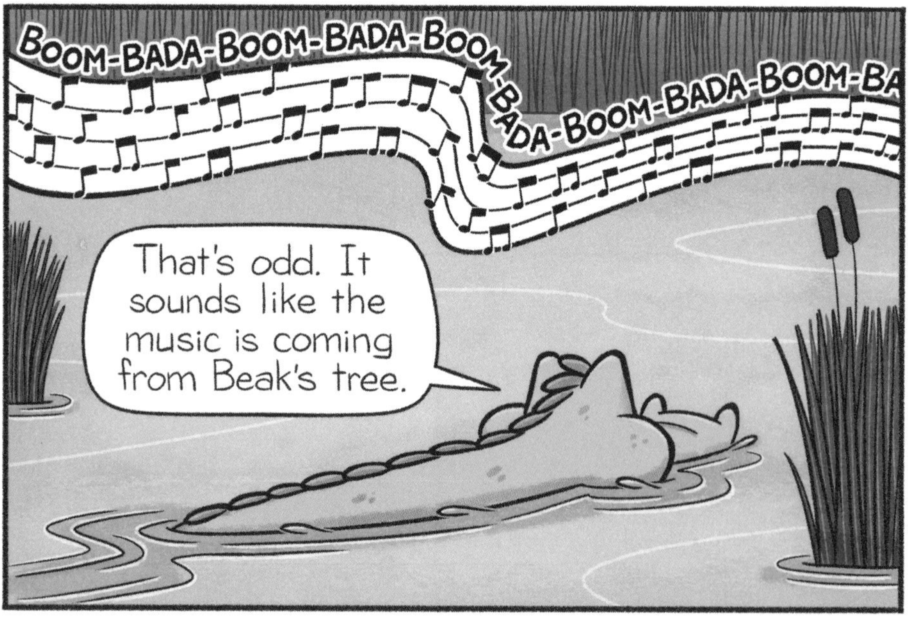
BOOM-BADA-BOOM-BADA-BOOM-BADA-BOOM-BADA-BOOM-BA
That's odd. It sounds like the music is coming from Beak's tree.

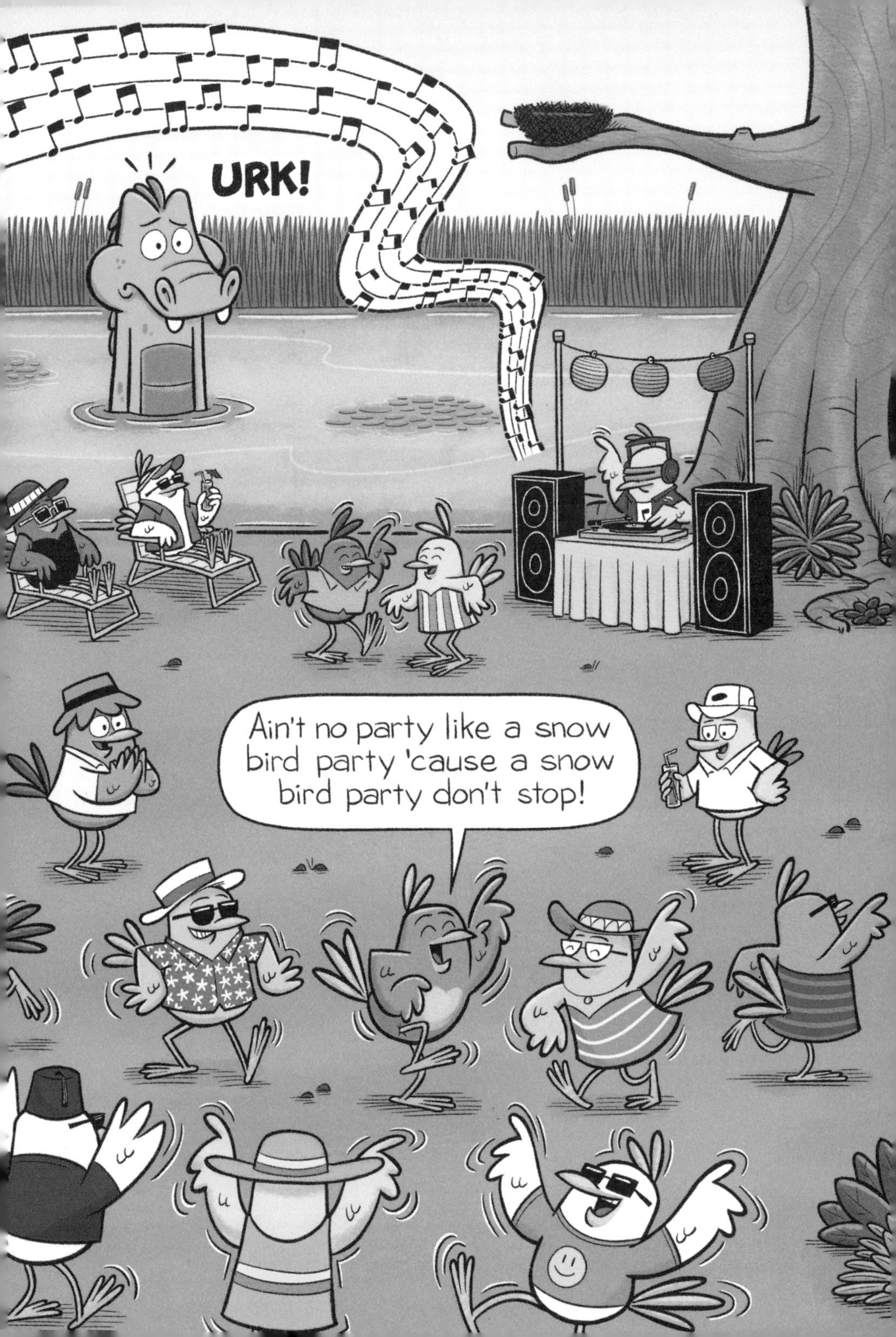
URK!
Ain't no party like a snow bird party 'cause a snow bird party don't stop!

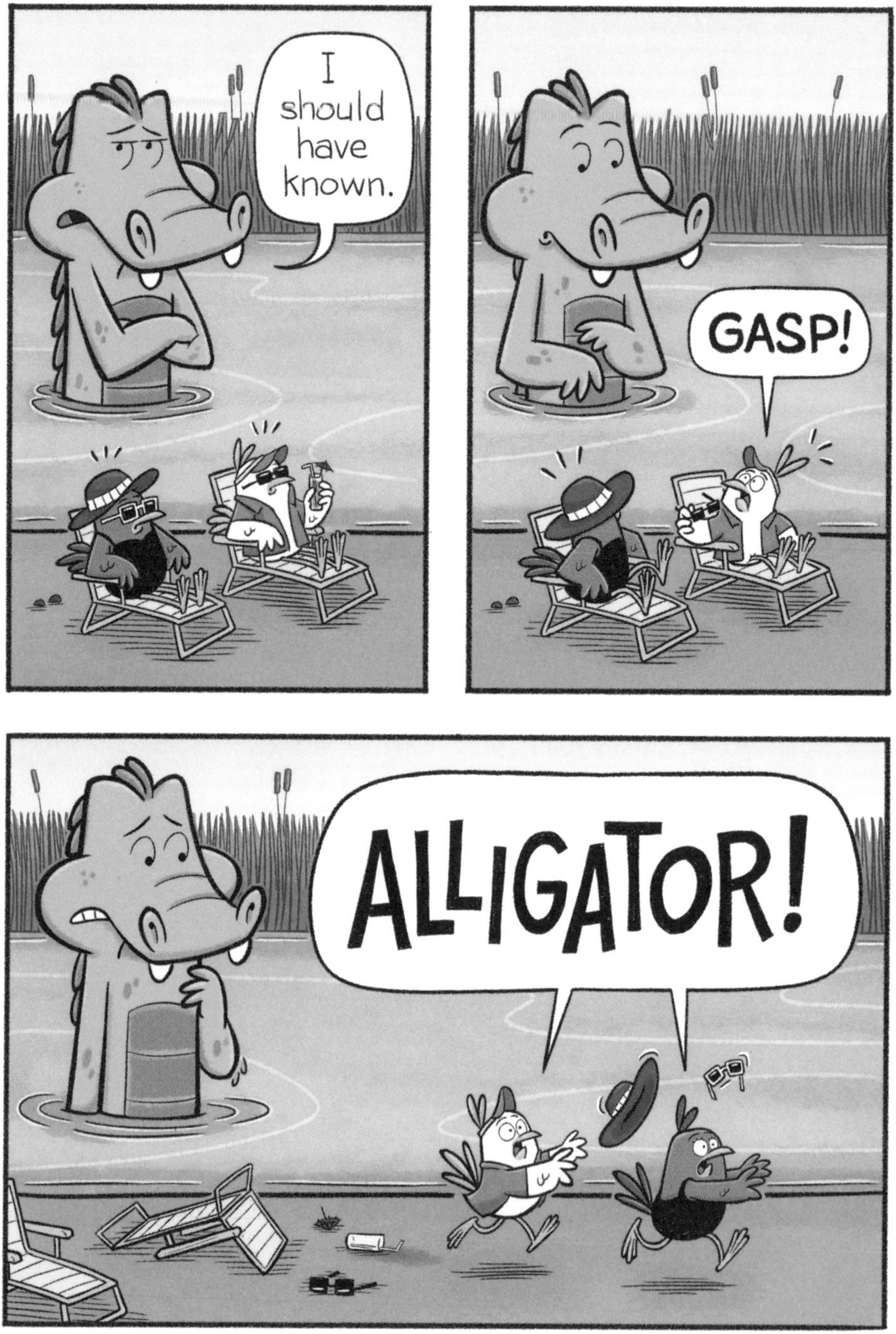
I should have known.
GASP!
ALLIGATOR!

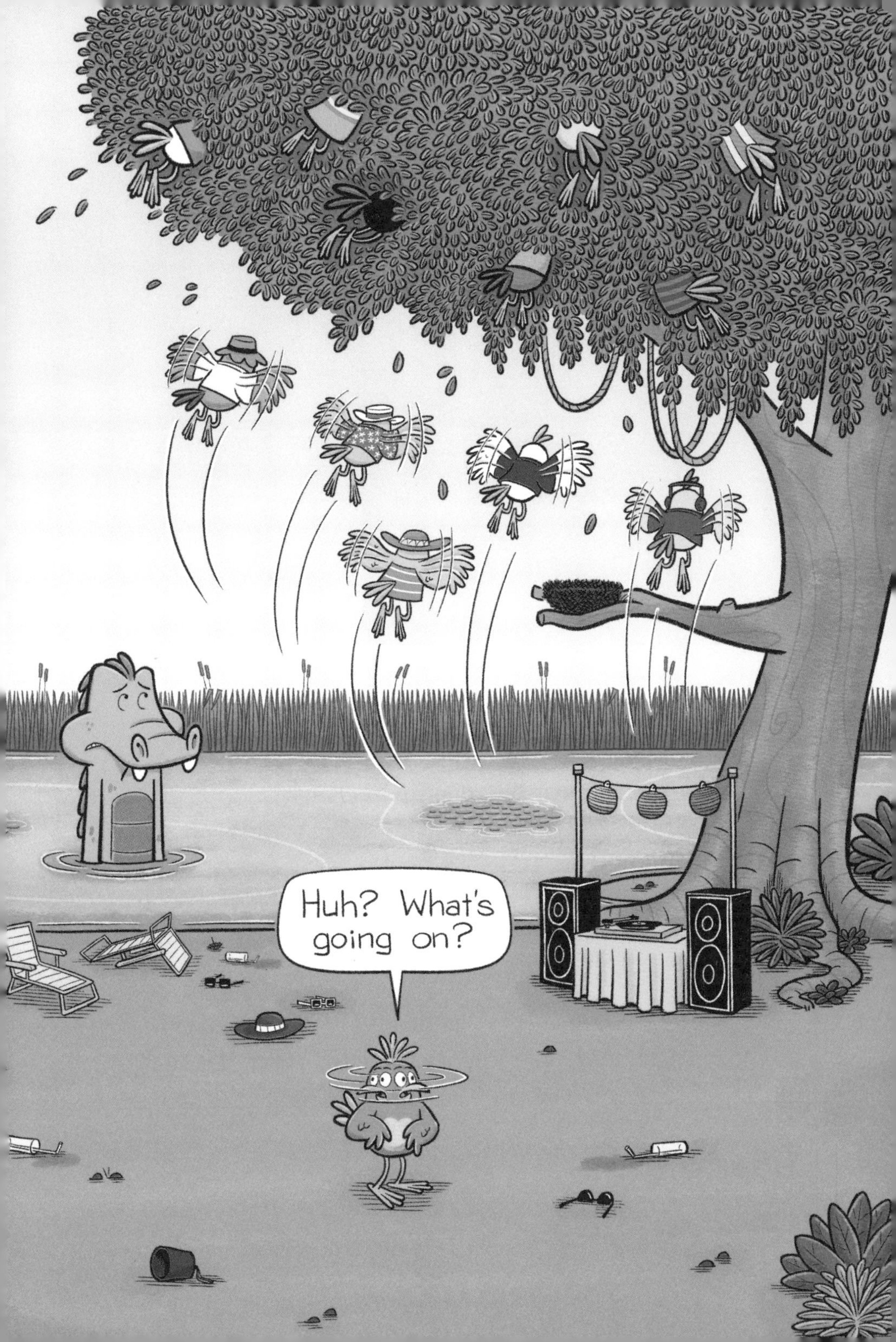
Huh? What's going on?

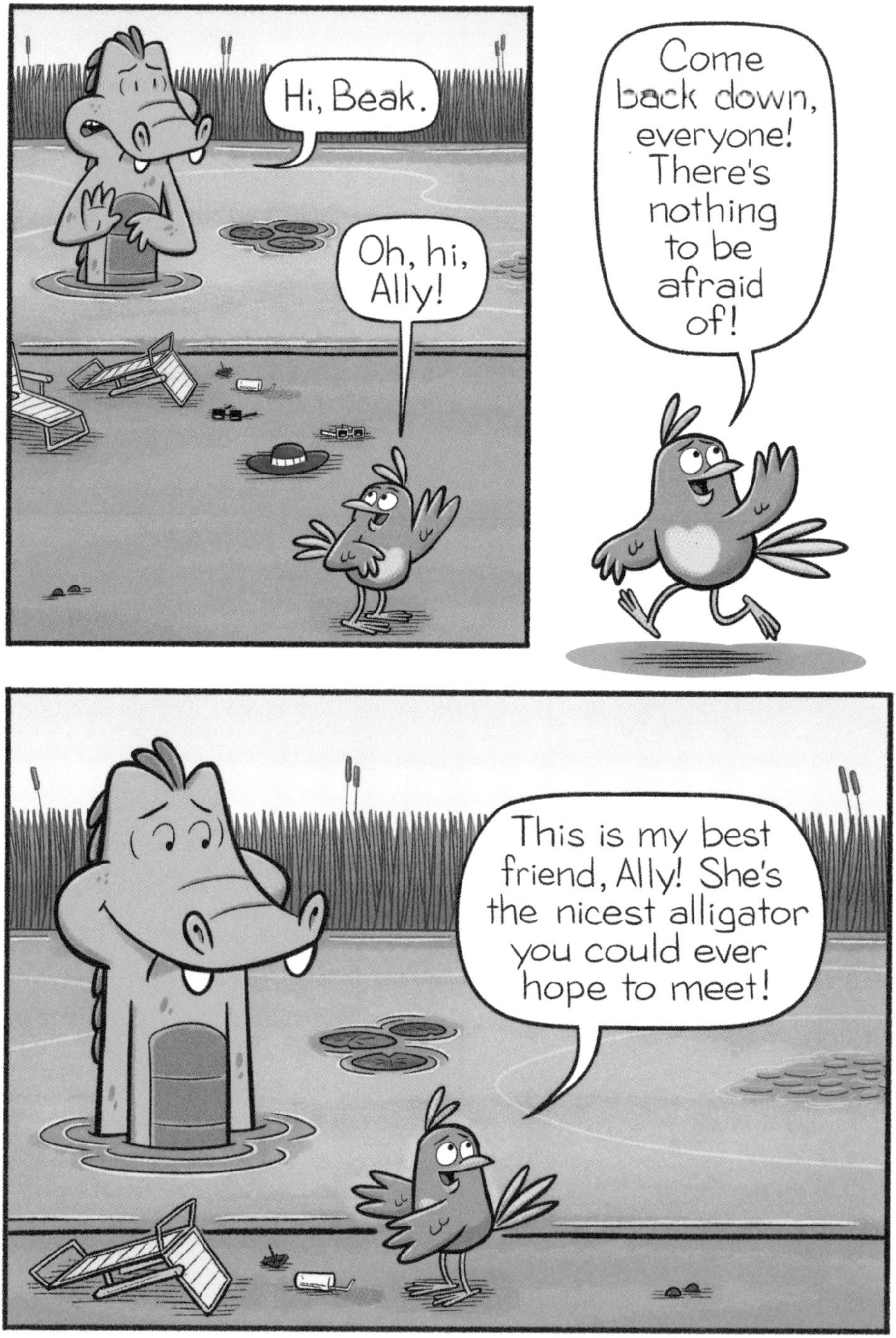
Hi, Beak.
Oh, hi, Ally!
Come back down, everyone! There's nothing to be afraid of!
This is my best friend, Ally! She's the nicest alligator you could ever hope to meet!

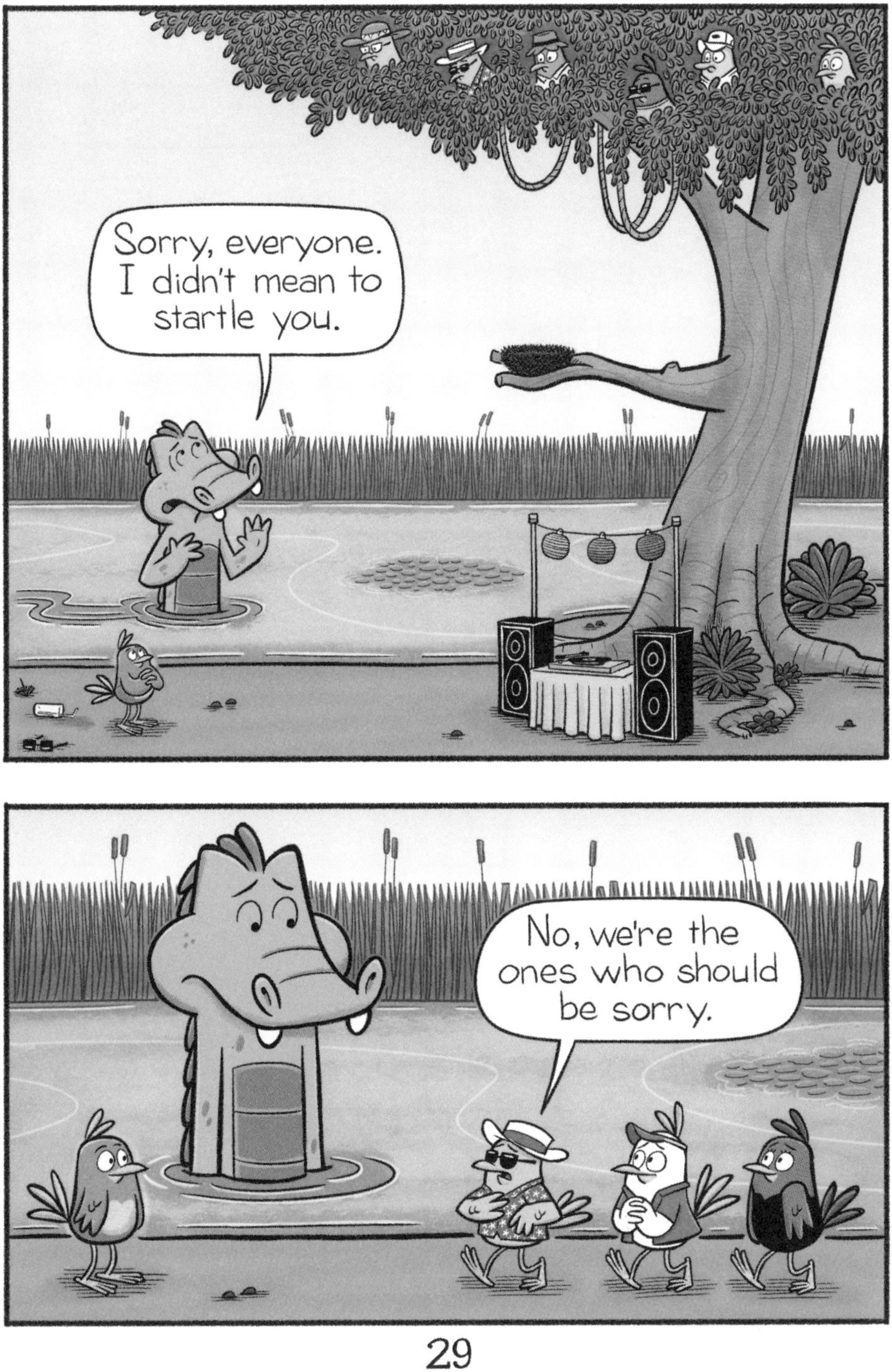
Sorry, everyone. I didn't mean to startle you.
No, we're the ones who should be sorry.

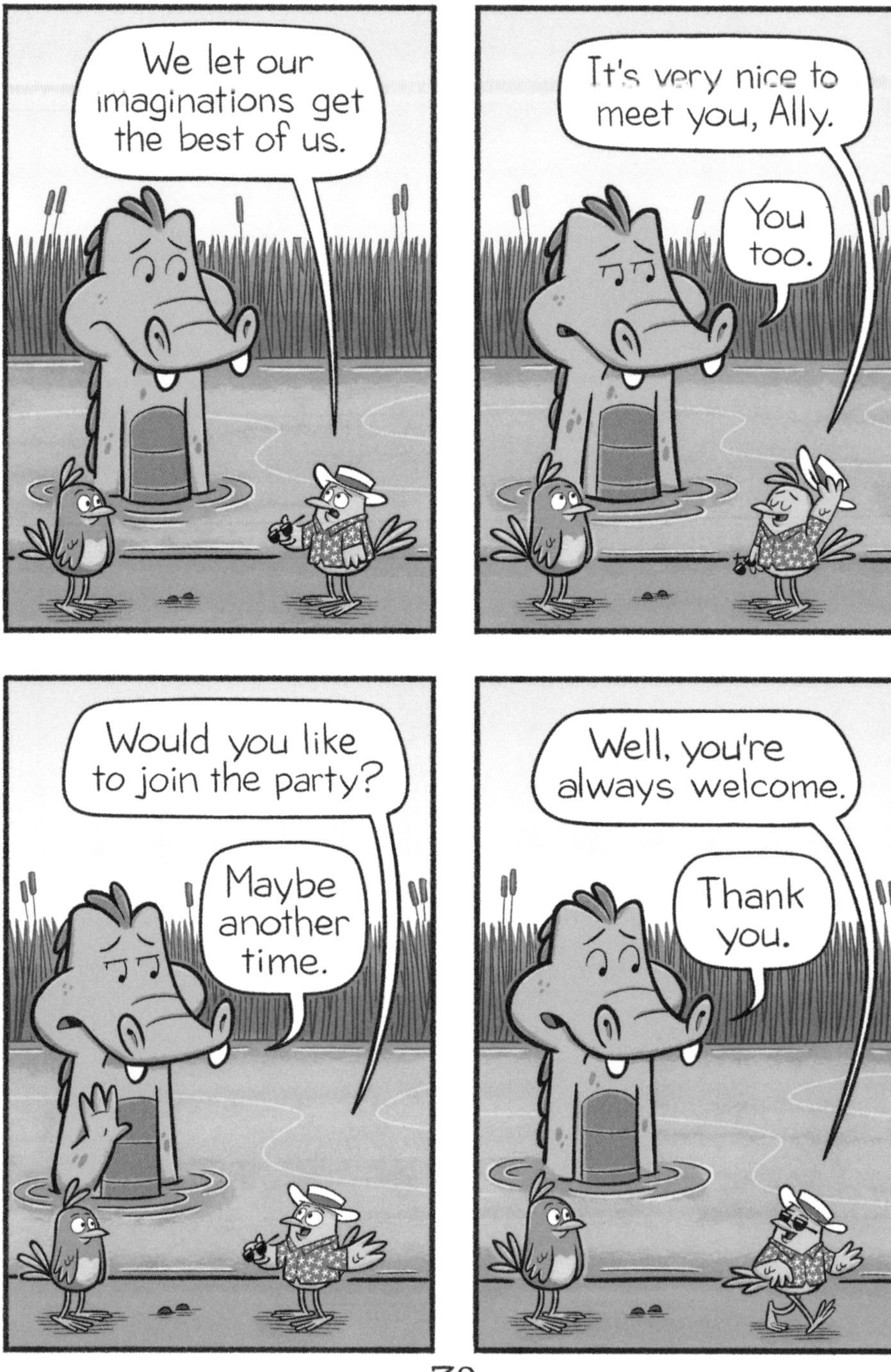
We let our imaginations get the best of us.
It's very nice to meet you, Ally.
You too.
Would you like to join the party?
Maybe another time.
Well, you're always welcome.
Thank you.

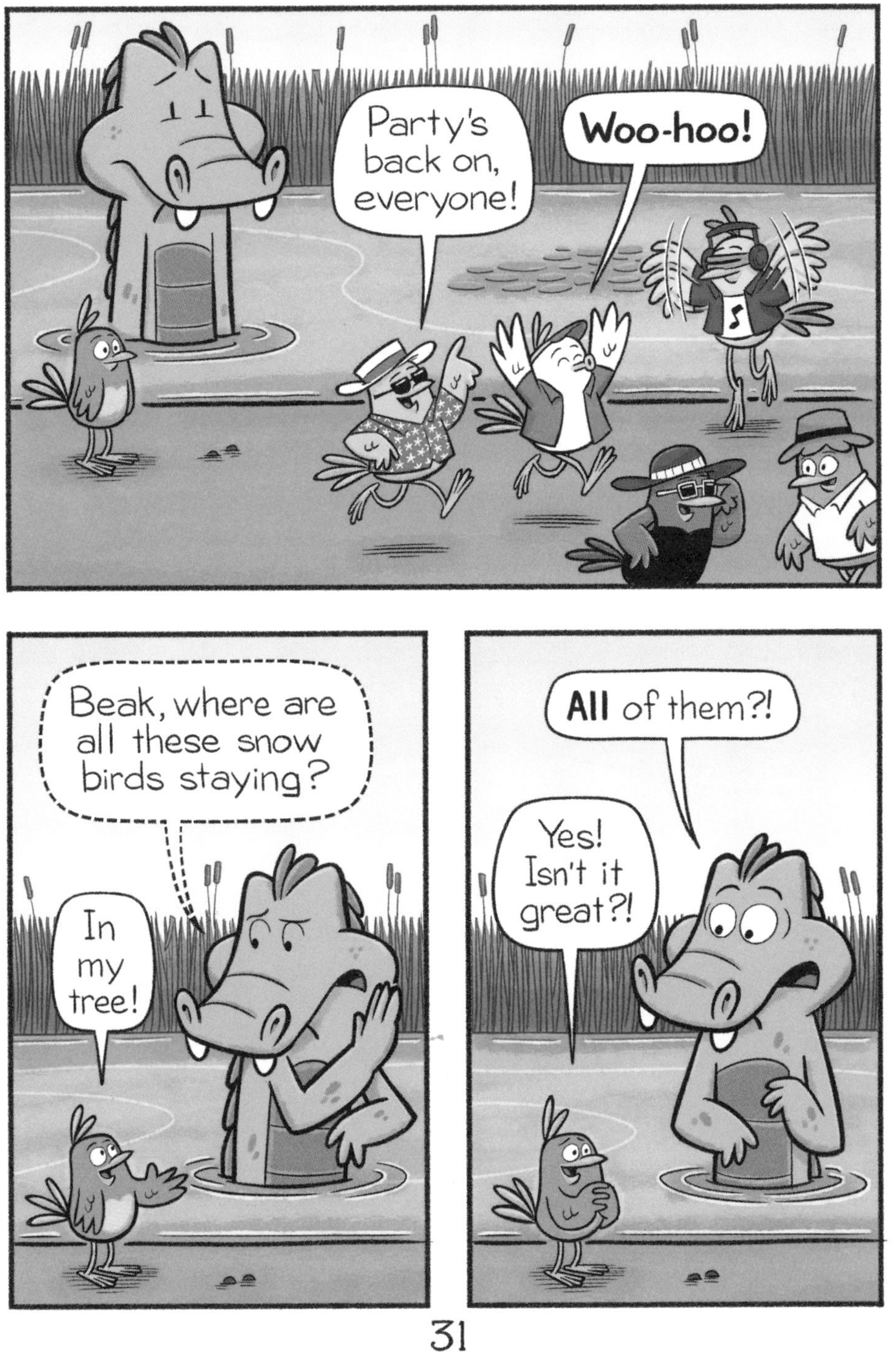
Party's back on, everyone!
Woo-hoo!
Beak, where are all these snow birds staying?
In my tree!
All of them?!
Yes! Isn't it great?!

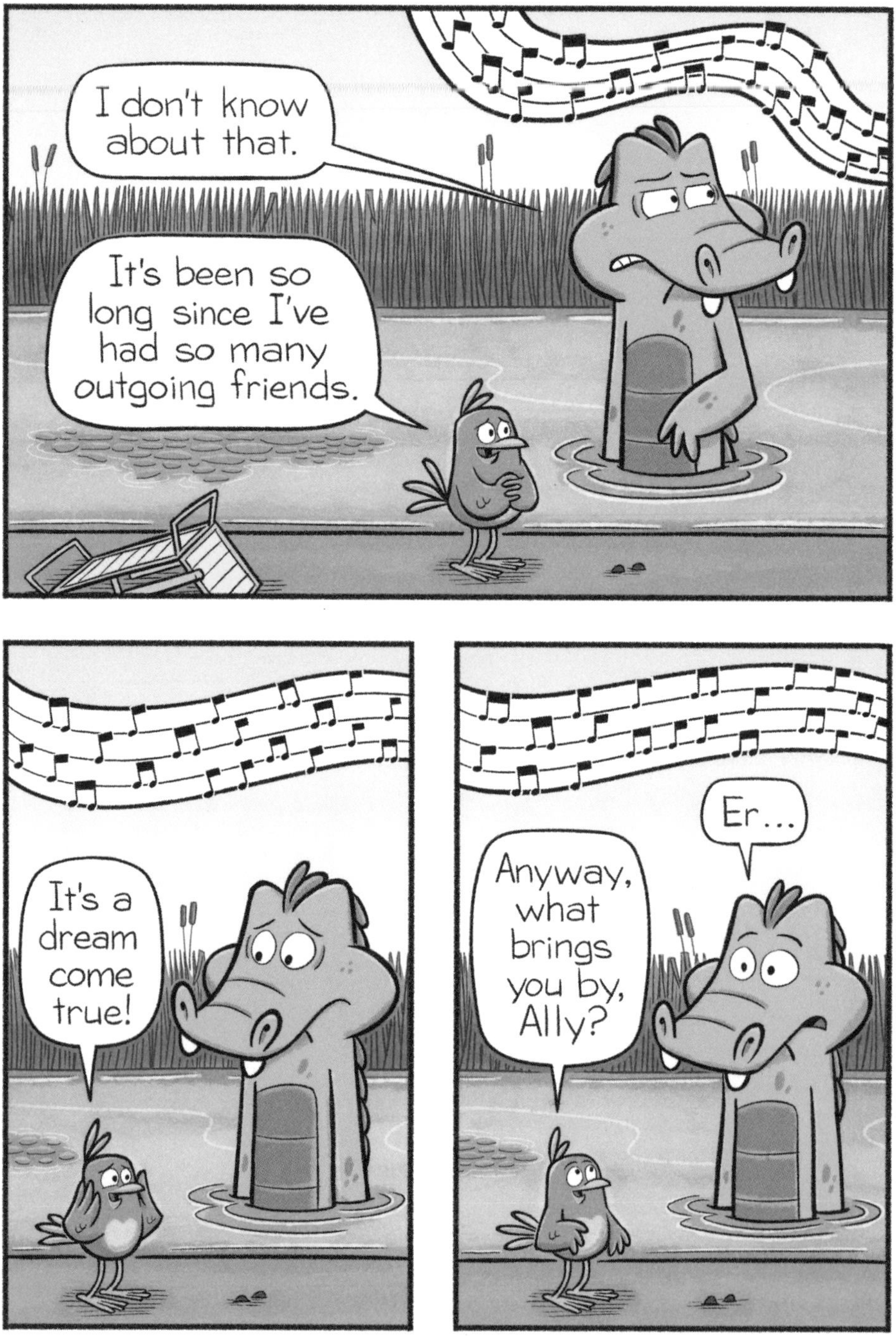
I don't know about that.
It's been so long since I've had so many outgoing friends.
It's a dream come true!
Er...
Anyway, what brings you by, Ally?

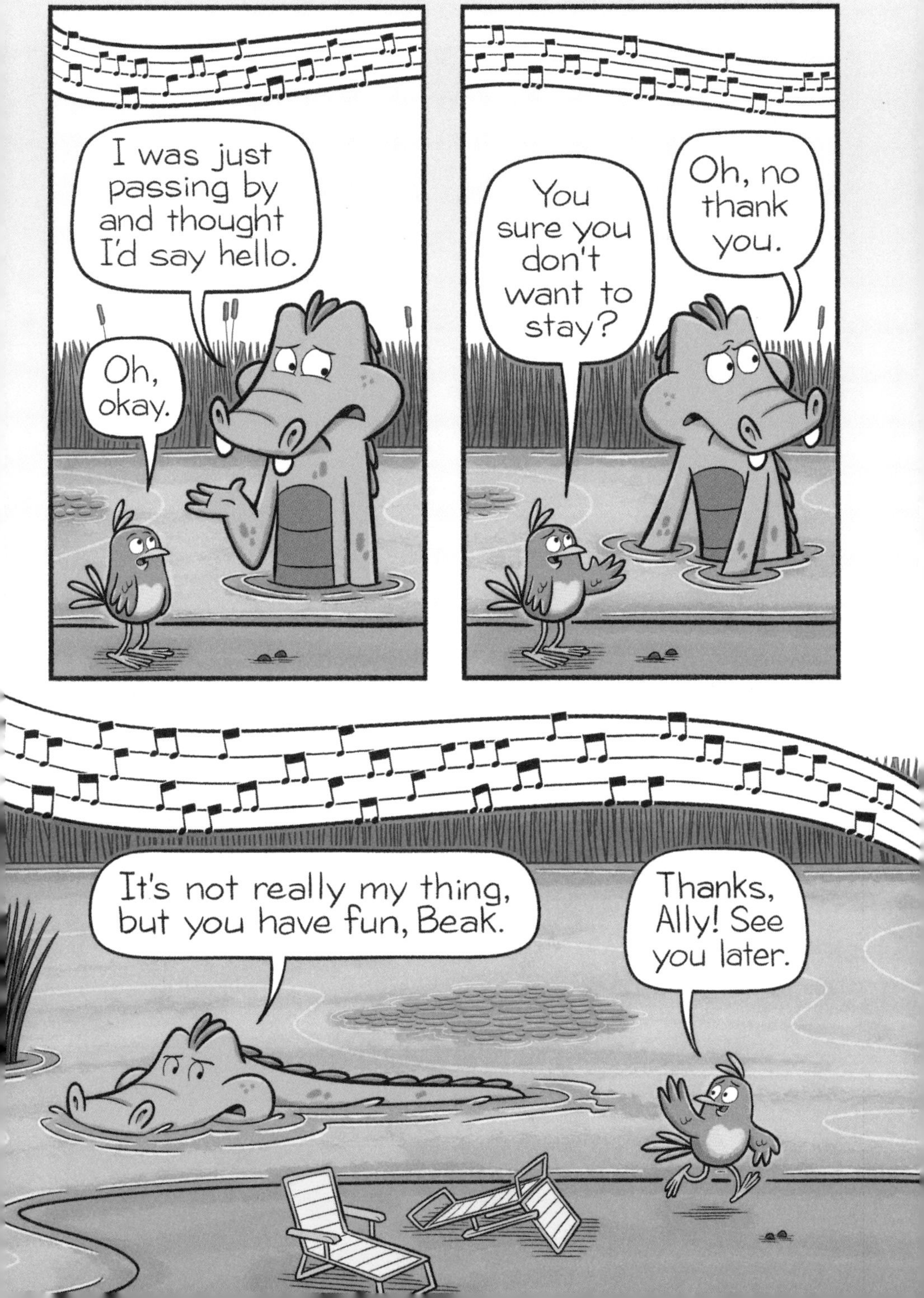
I was just passing by and thought I'd say hello.
Oh, okay.
You sure you don't want to stay?
Oh, no thank you.
It's not really my thing, but you have fun, Beak.
Thanks, Ally! See you later.

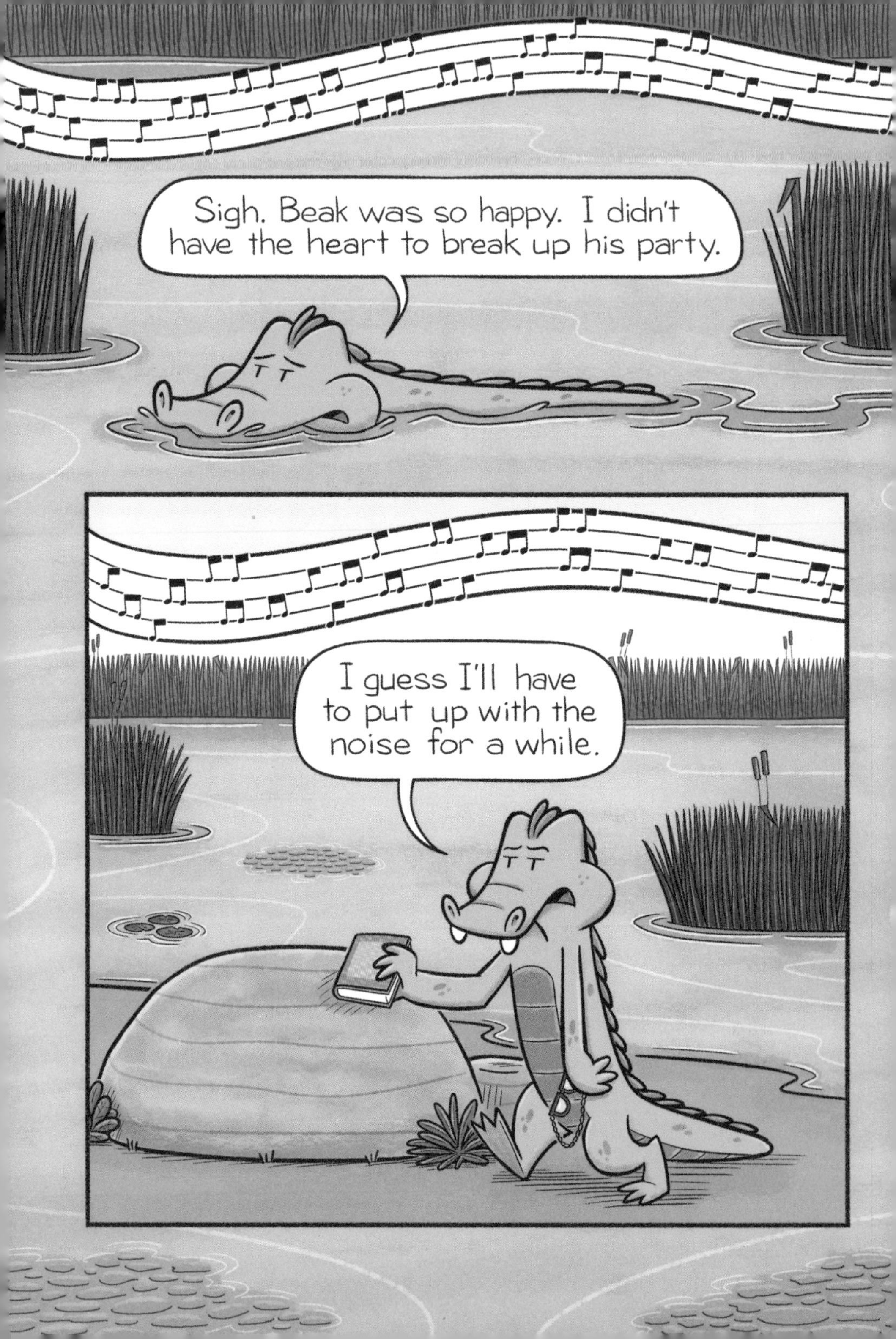
Sigh. Beak was so happy. I didn't have the heart to break up his party.
I guess I'll have to put up with the noise for a while.

The things I do for that bird.

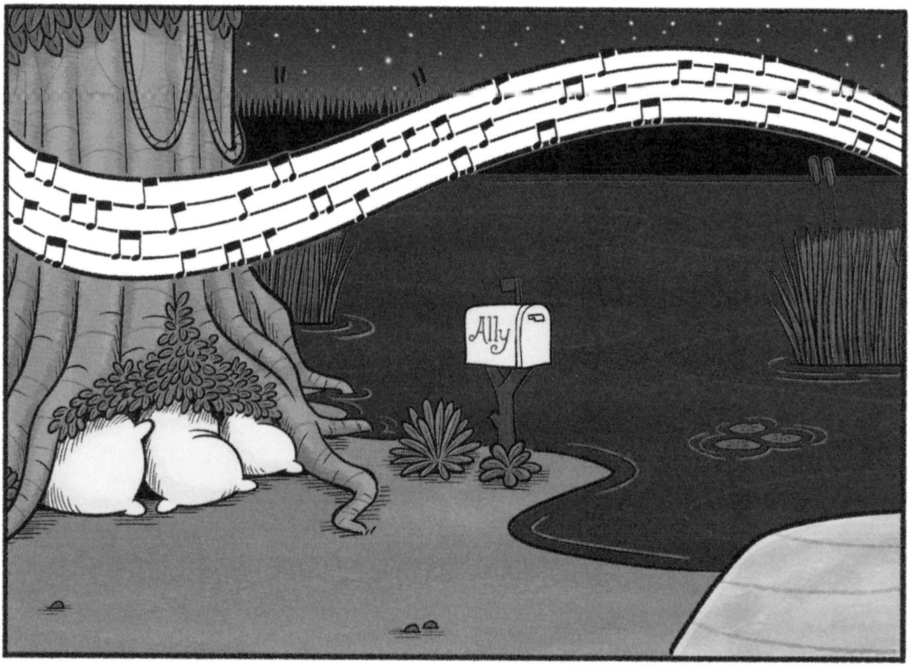
Ally

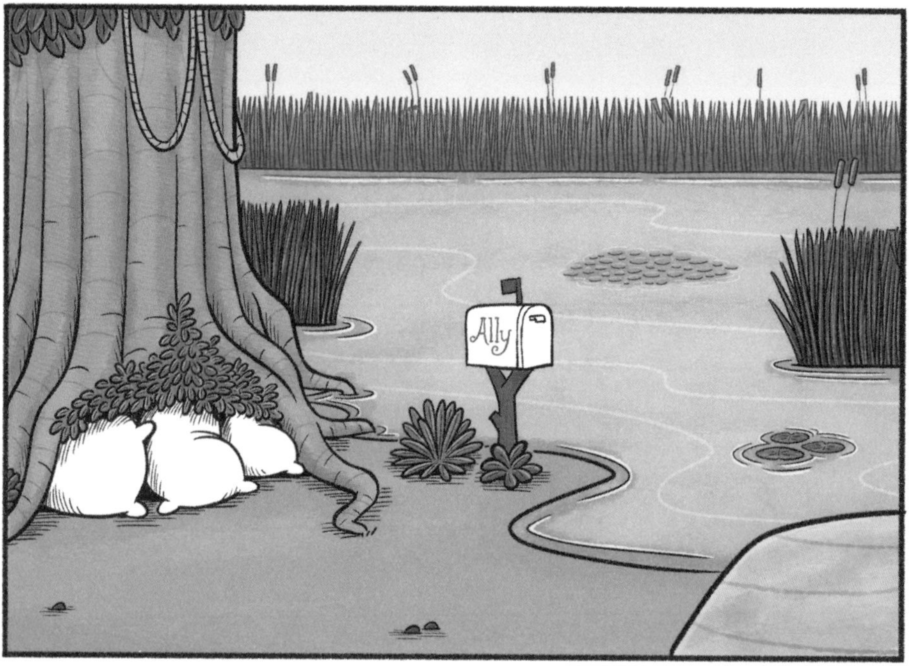
Ally

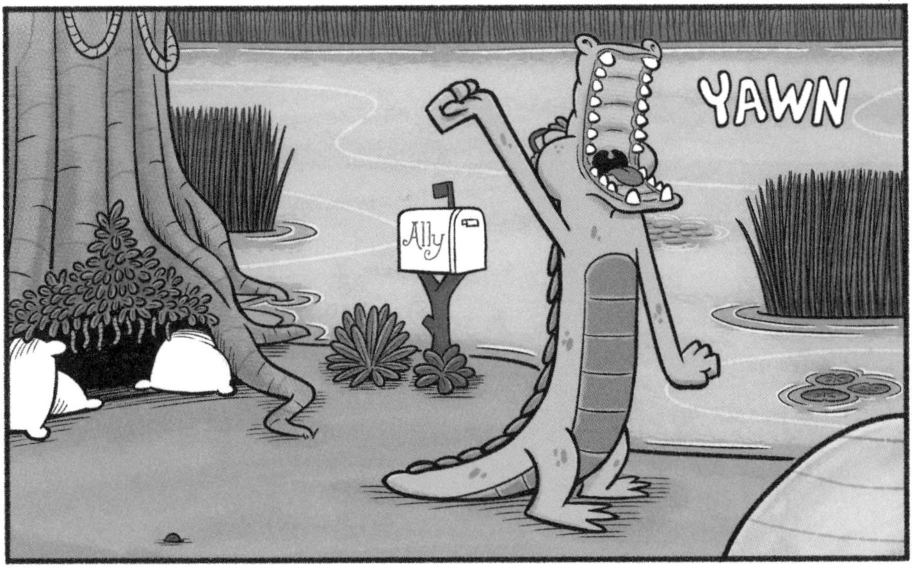
Ally
YAWN

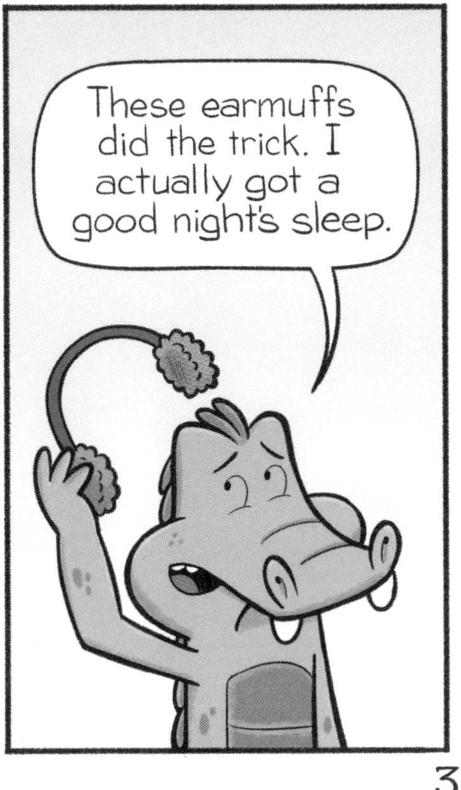
These earmuffs did the trick. I actually got a good night's sleep.

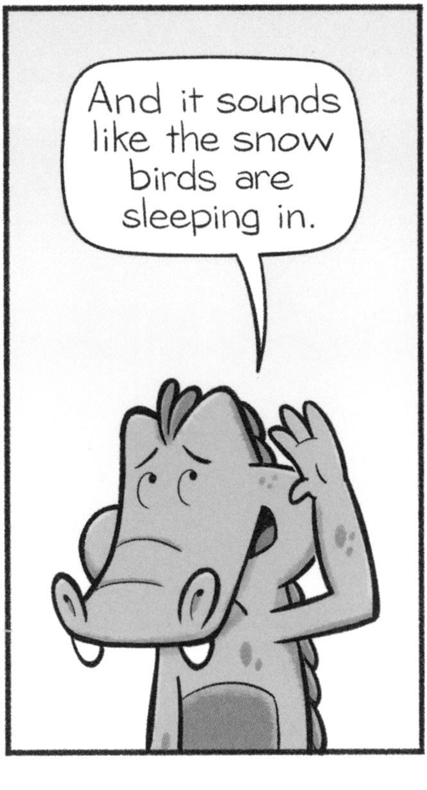
And it sounds like the snow birds are sleeping in.

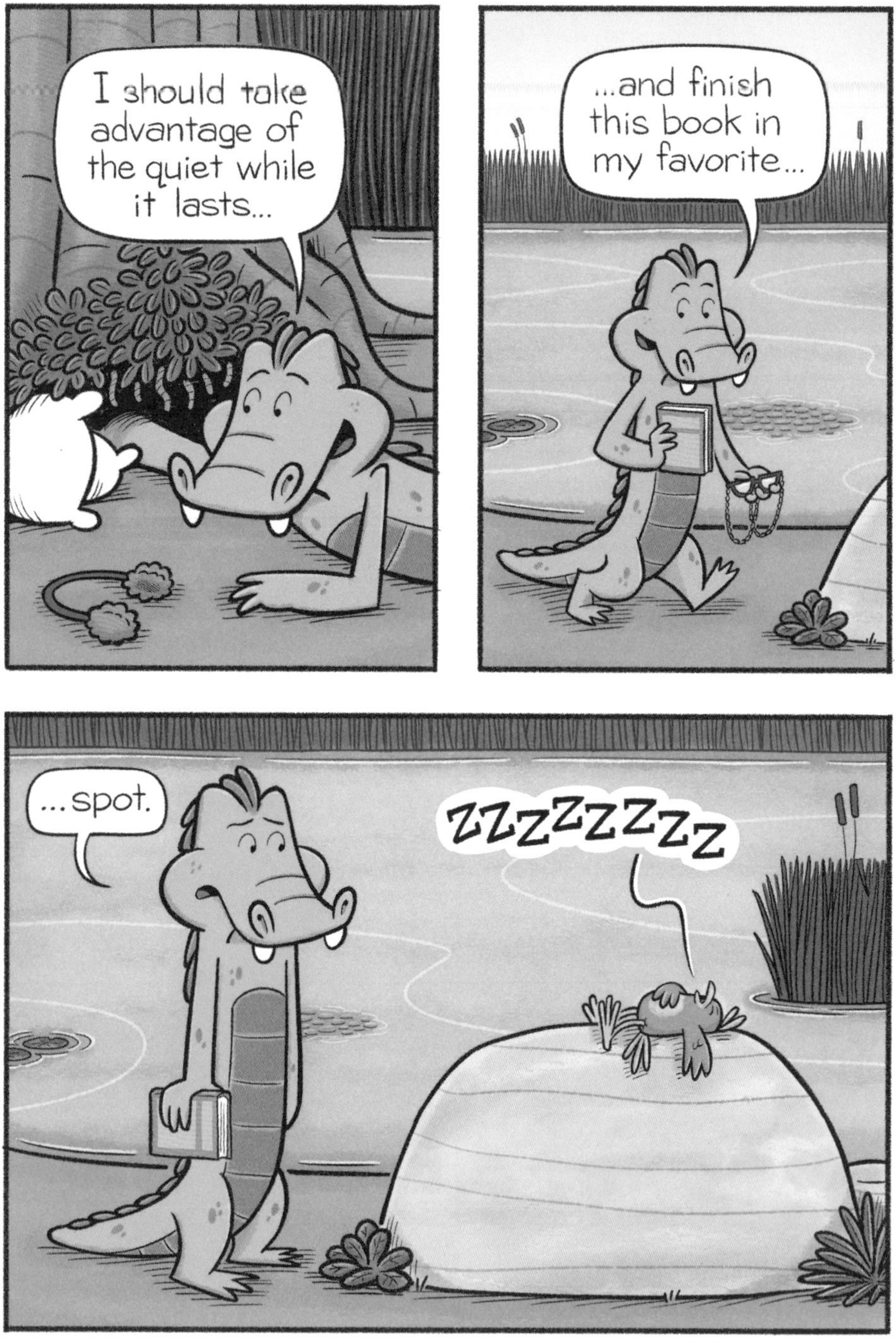
I should take advantage of the quiet while it lasts...
...and finish this book in my favorite...
...spot.
ZZZZZZZZ

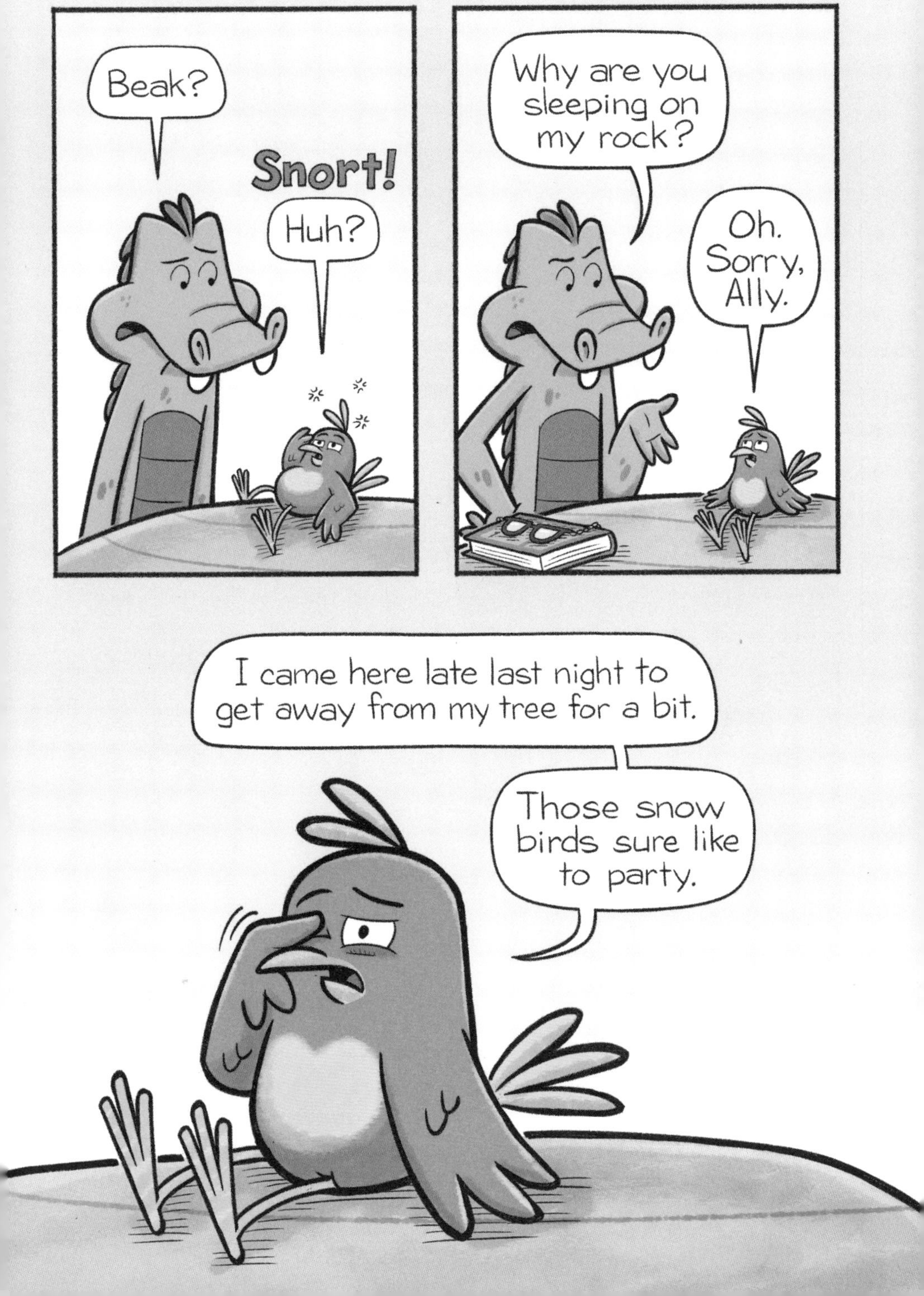
Beak?
Snort!
Huh?
Why are you sleeping on my rock?
Oh. Sorry, Ally.
I came here late last night to get away from my tree for a bit.
Those snow birds sure like to party.

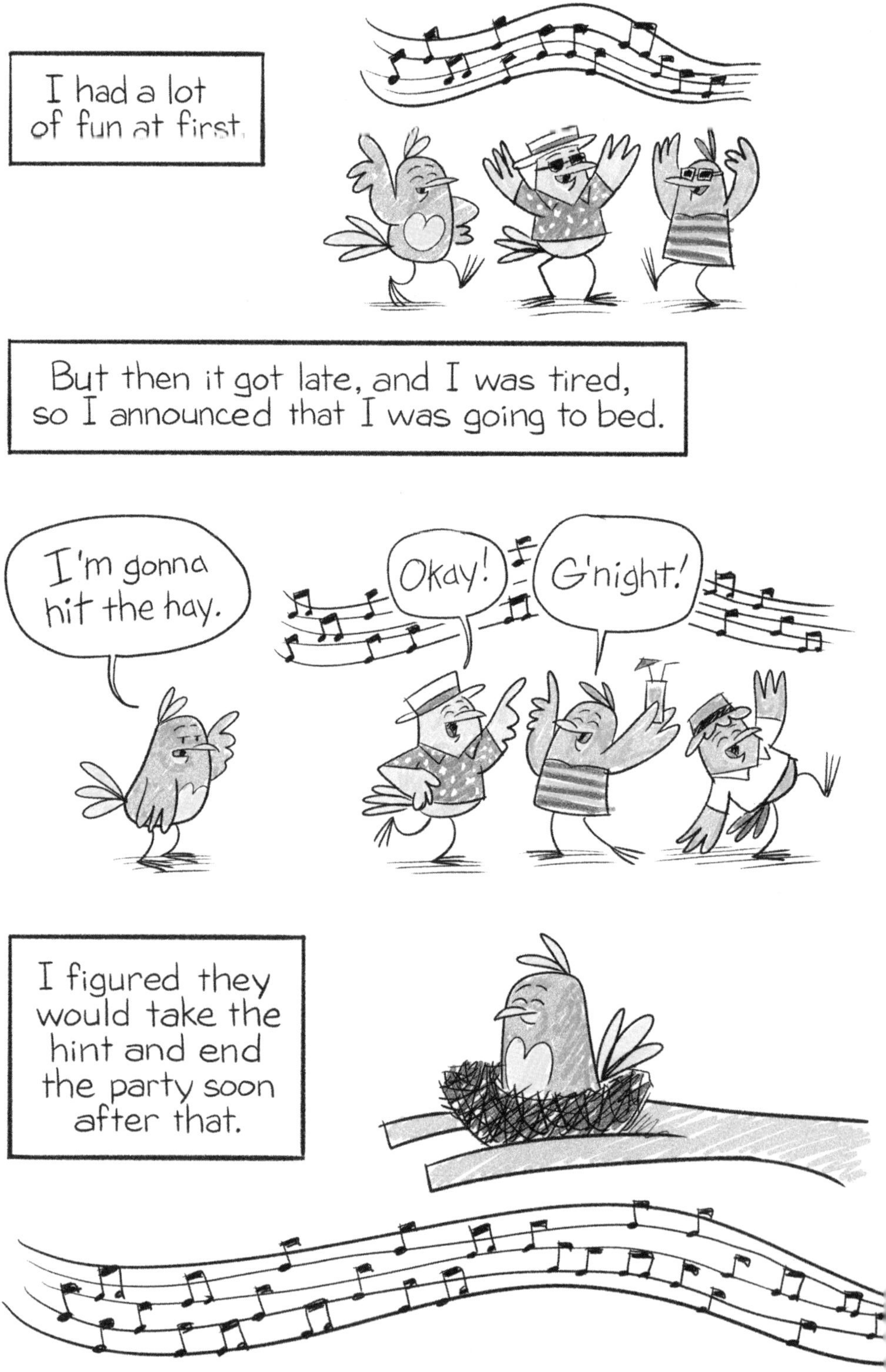
I had a lot of fun at first.
But then it got late, and I was tired, so I announced that I was going to bed.
I'm gonna hit the hay.
Okay!
G'night!
I figured they would take the hint and end the party soon after that.

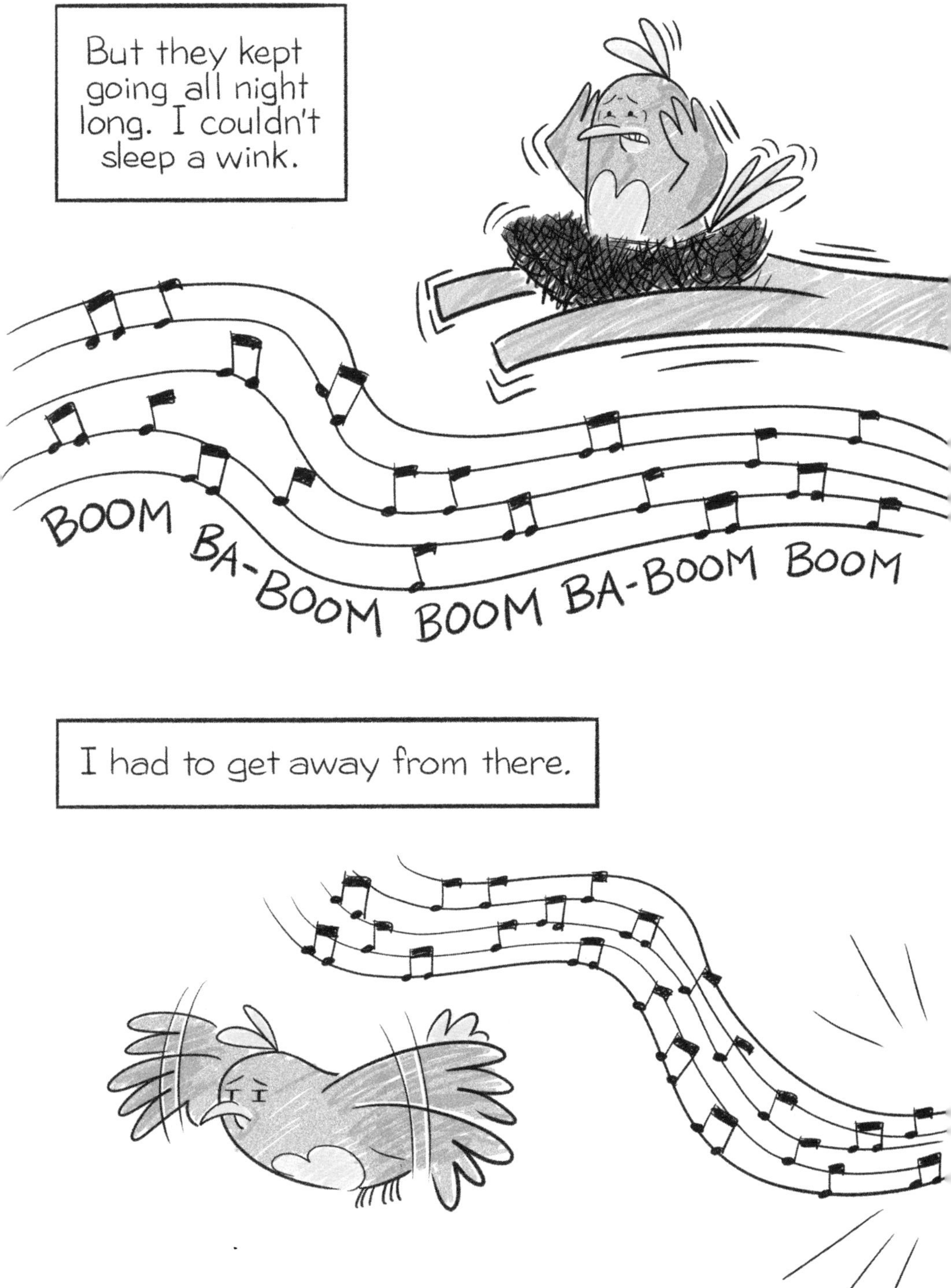
But they kept going all night long. I couldn't sleep a wink.
BOOM BA-BOOM BOOM BA-BOOM BOOM
I had to get away from there.

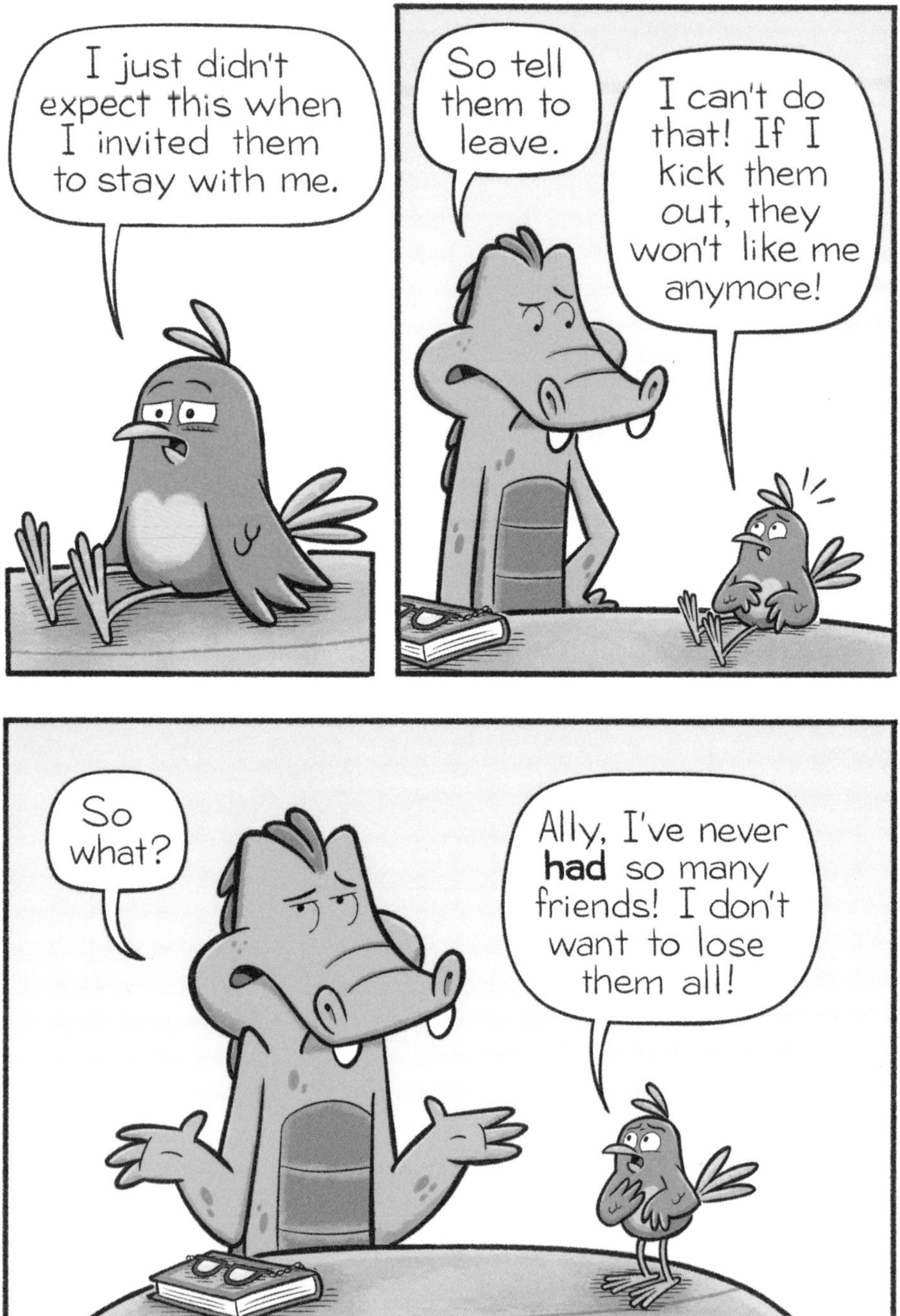
I just didn't expect this when I invited them to stay with me.
So tell them to leave.
I can't do that! If I kick them out, they won't like me anymore!
So what?
Ally, I've never **had** so many friends! I don't want to lose them all!

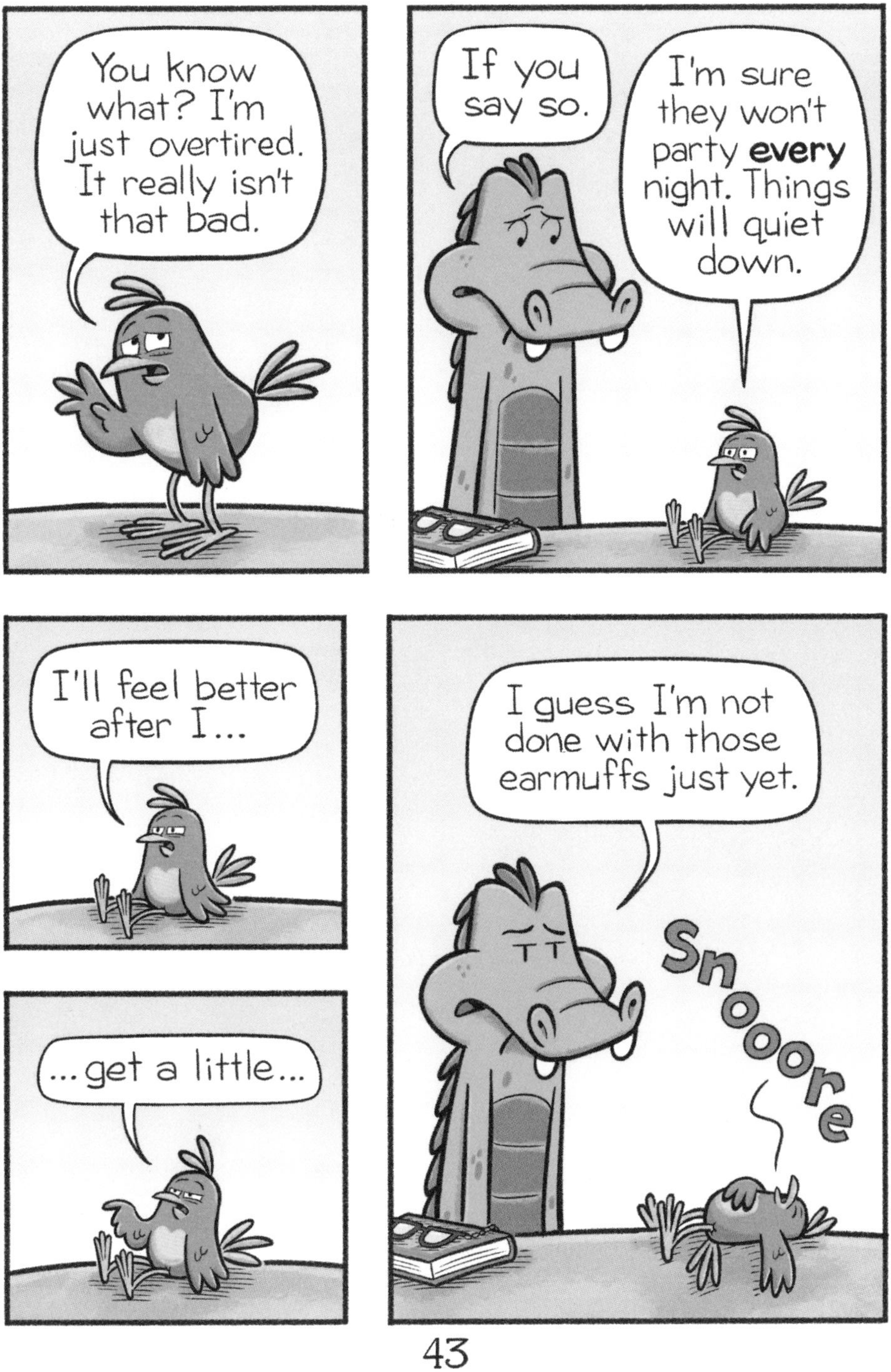
You know what? I'm just overtired. It really isn't that bad.
If you say so.
I'm sure they won't party **every** night. Things will quiet down.
I'll feel better after I...
...get a little...
I guess I'm not done with those earmuffs just yet.
Snooore

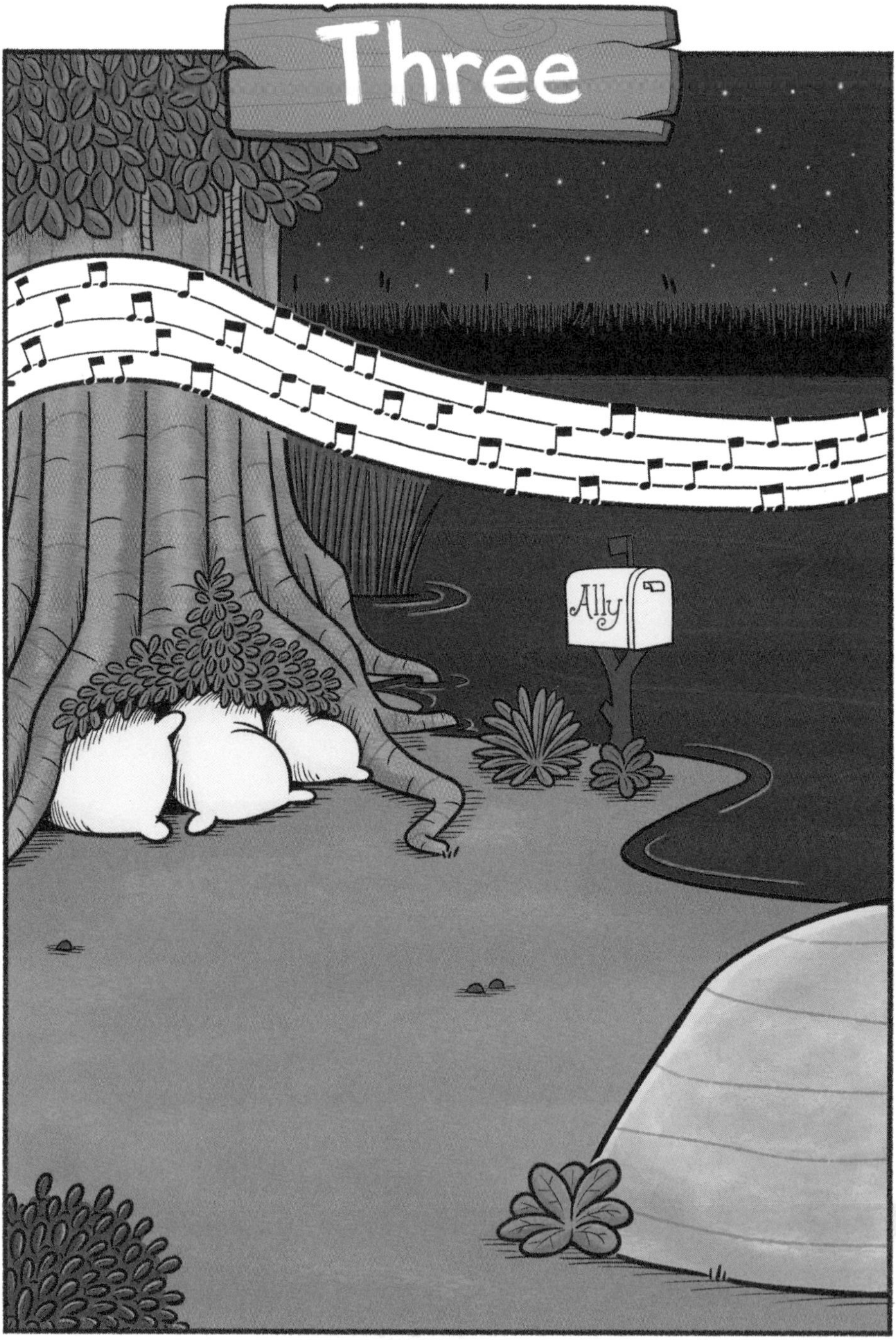
Three
Ally

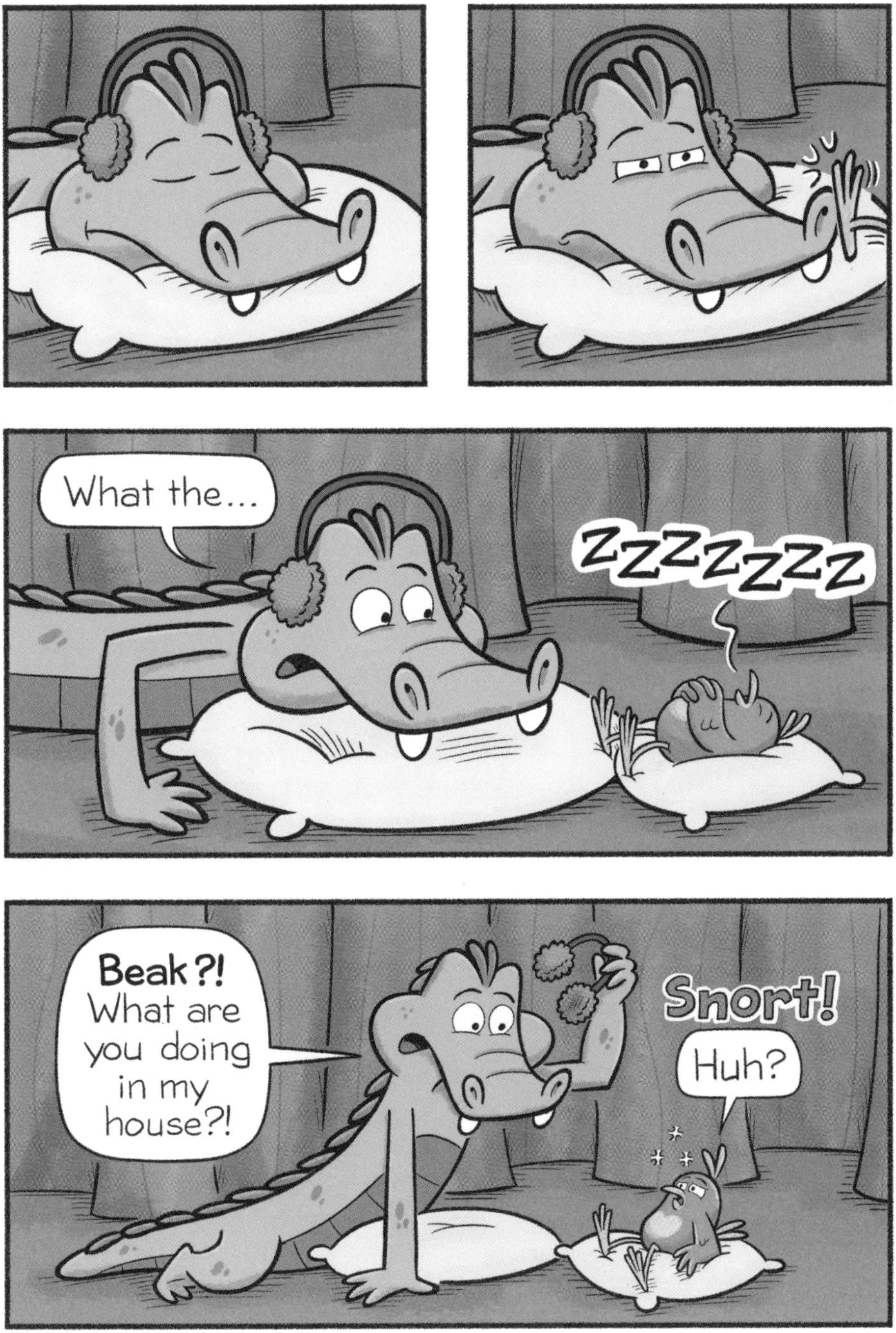

What the...
ZZZZZZZZ
Beak?!
What are you doing in my house?!
Snort!
Huh?

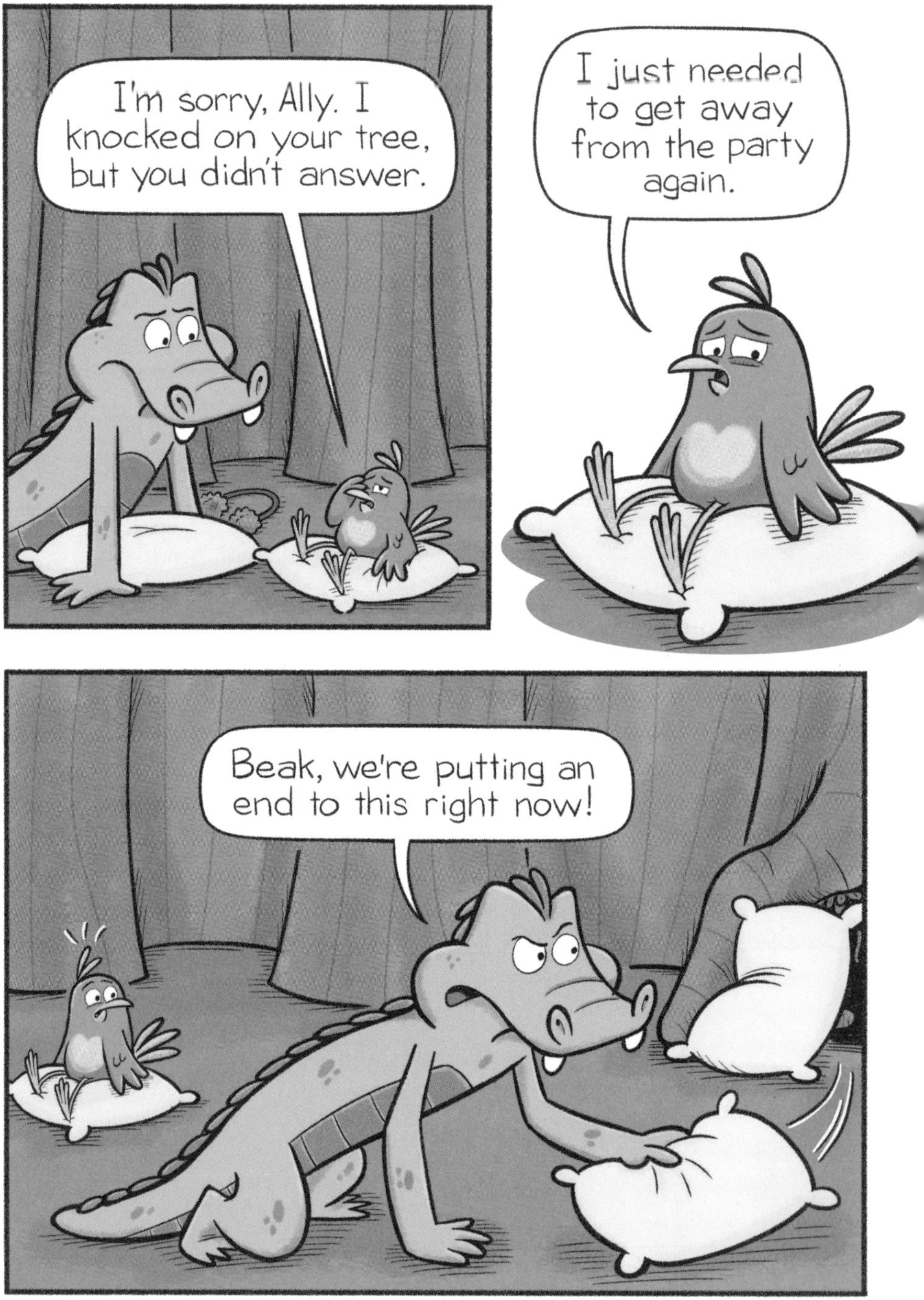
I'm sorry, Ally. I knocked on your tree, but you didn't answer.
I just needed to get away from the party again.
Beak, we're putting an end to this right now!

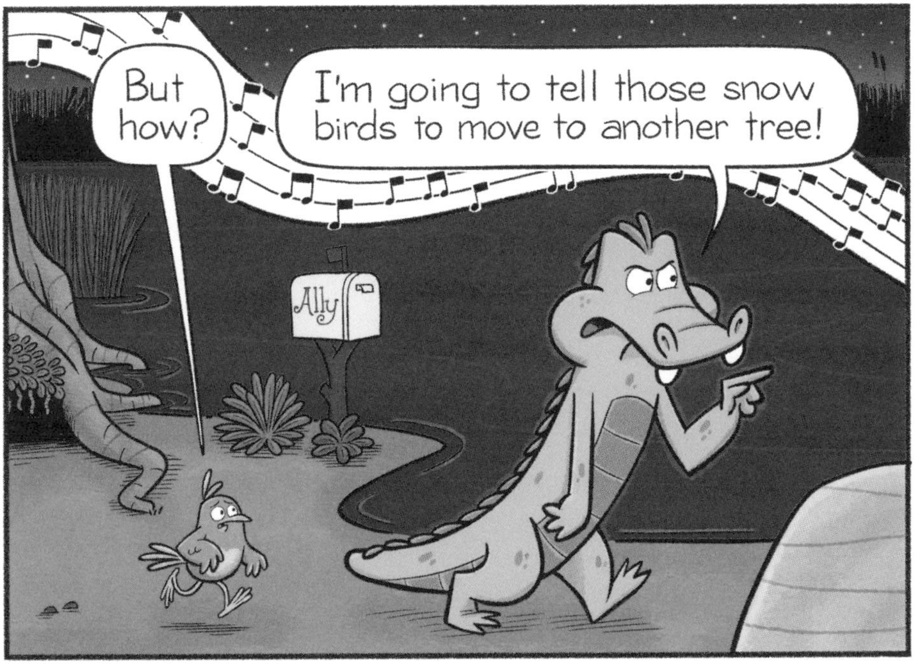
But how?
I'm going to tell those snow birds to move to another tree!
Ally

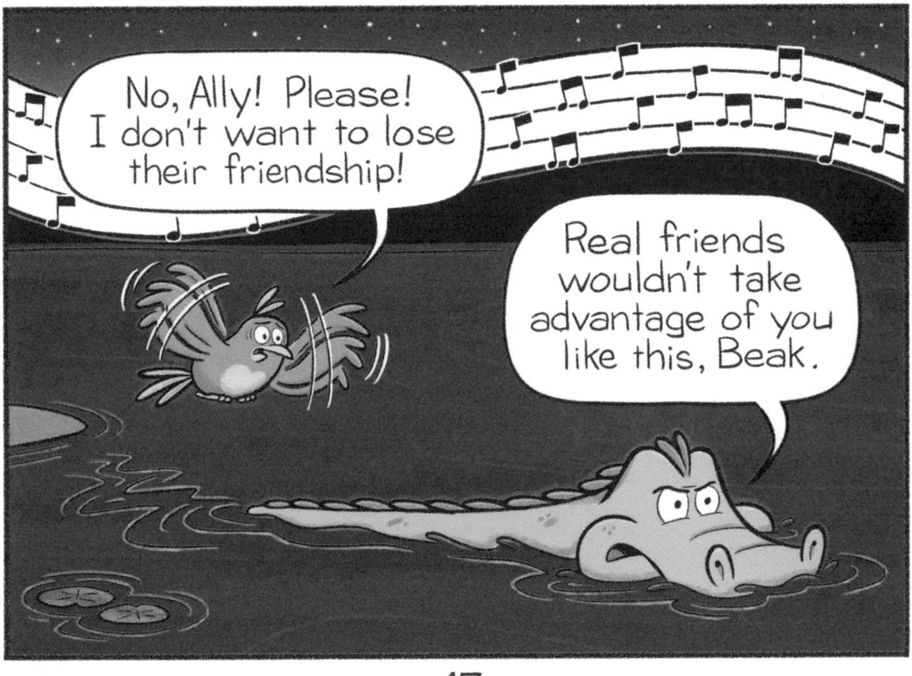
No, Ally! Please! I don't want to lose their friendship!
Real friends wouldn't take advantage of you like this, Beak.

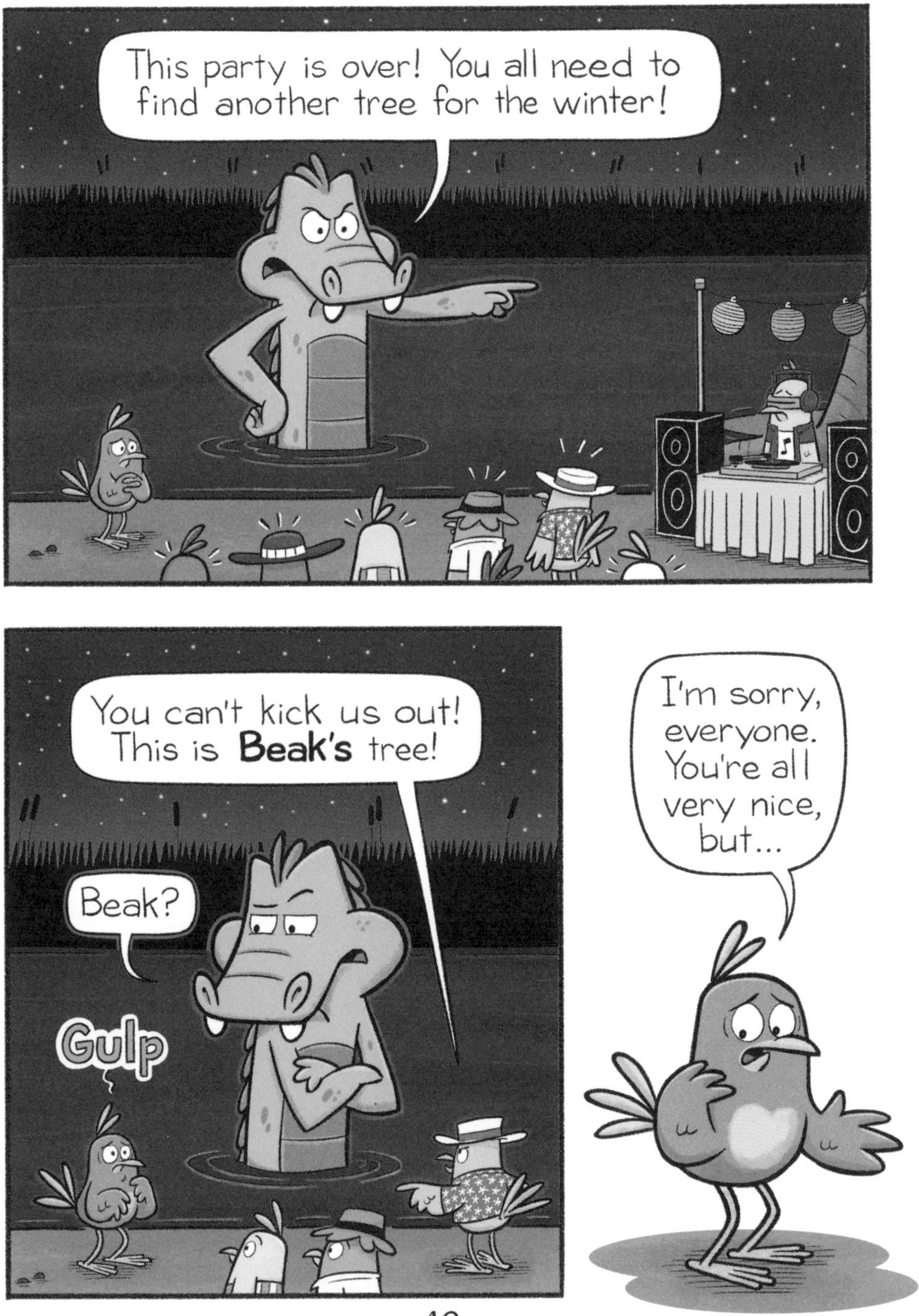
This party is over! You all need to find another tree for the winter!
You can't kick us out! This is **Beak's** tree!
Beak?
Gulp
I'm sorry, everyone. You're all very nice, but...

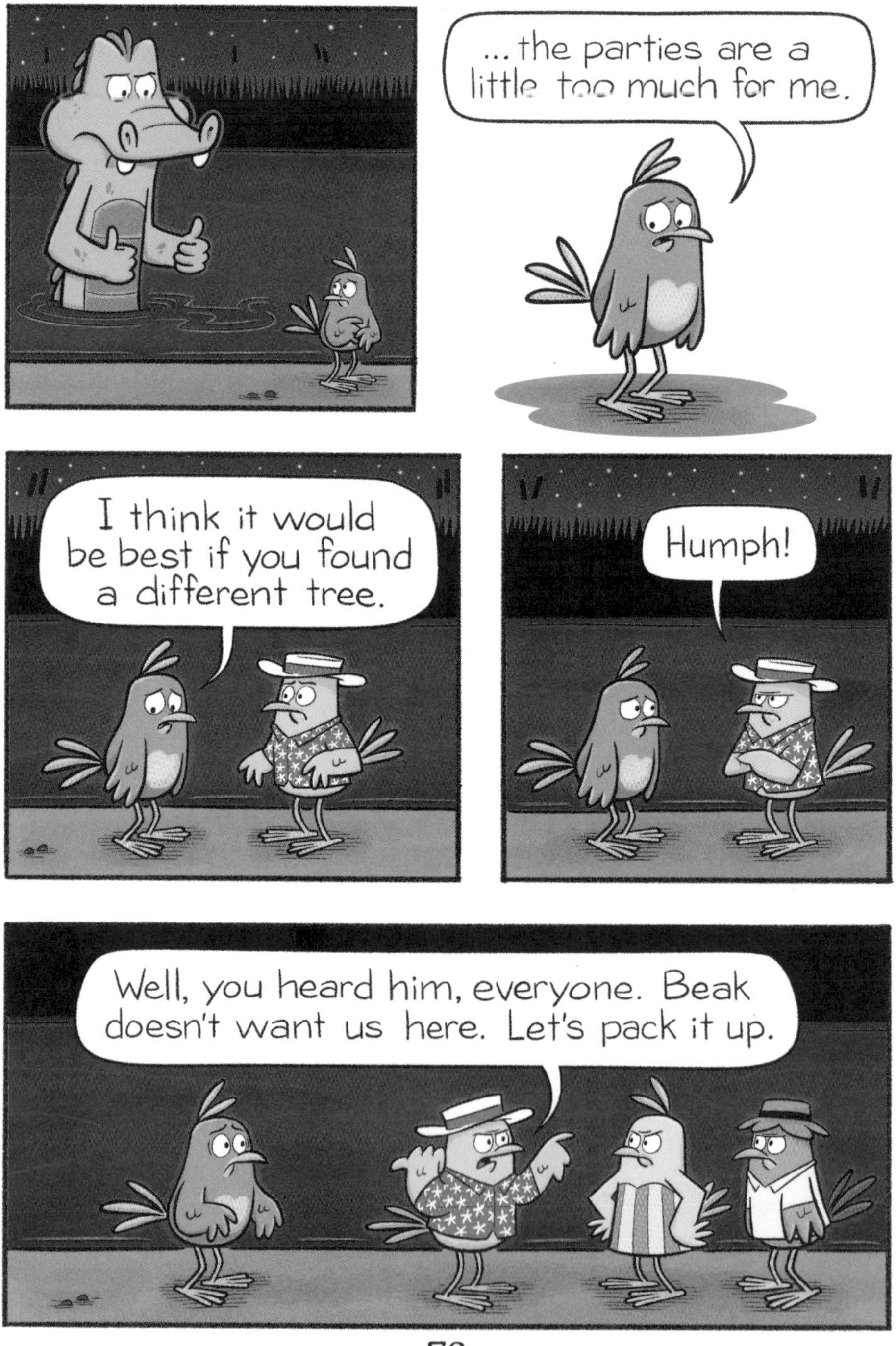

...the parties are a little too much for me.
I think it would be best if you found a different tree.
Humph!
Well, you heard him, everyone. Beak doesn't want us here. Let's pack it up.

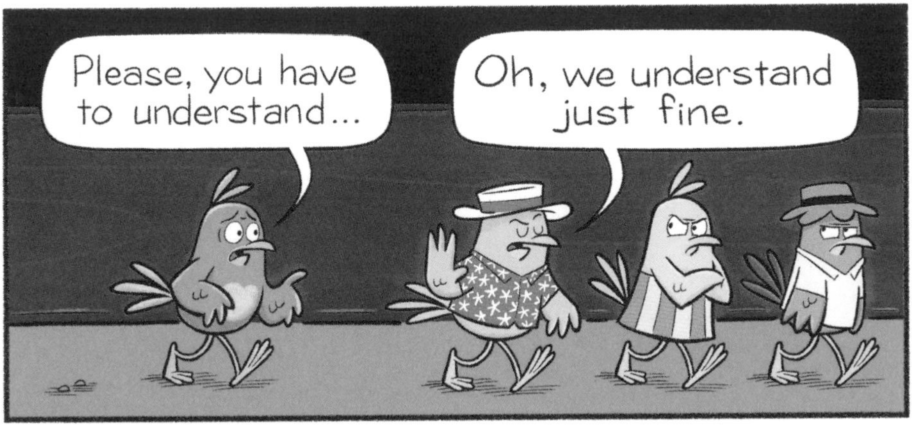
Please, you have to understand...
Oh, we understand just fine.

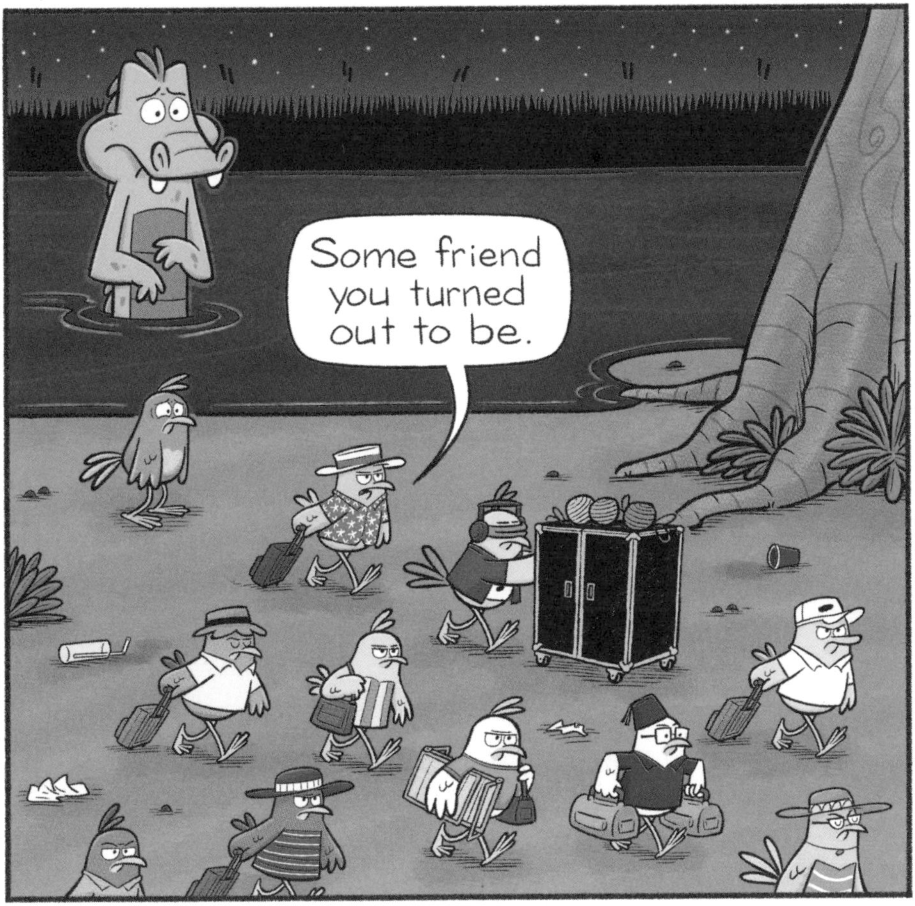
Some friend you turned out to be.

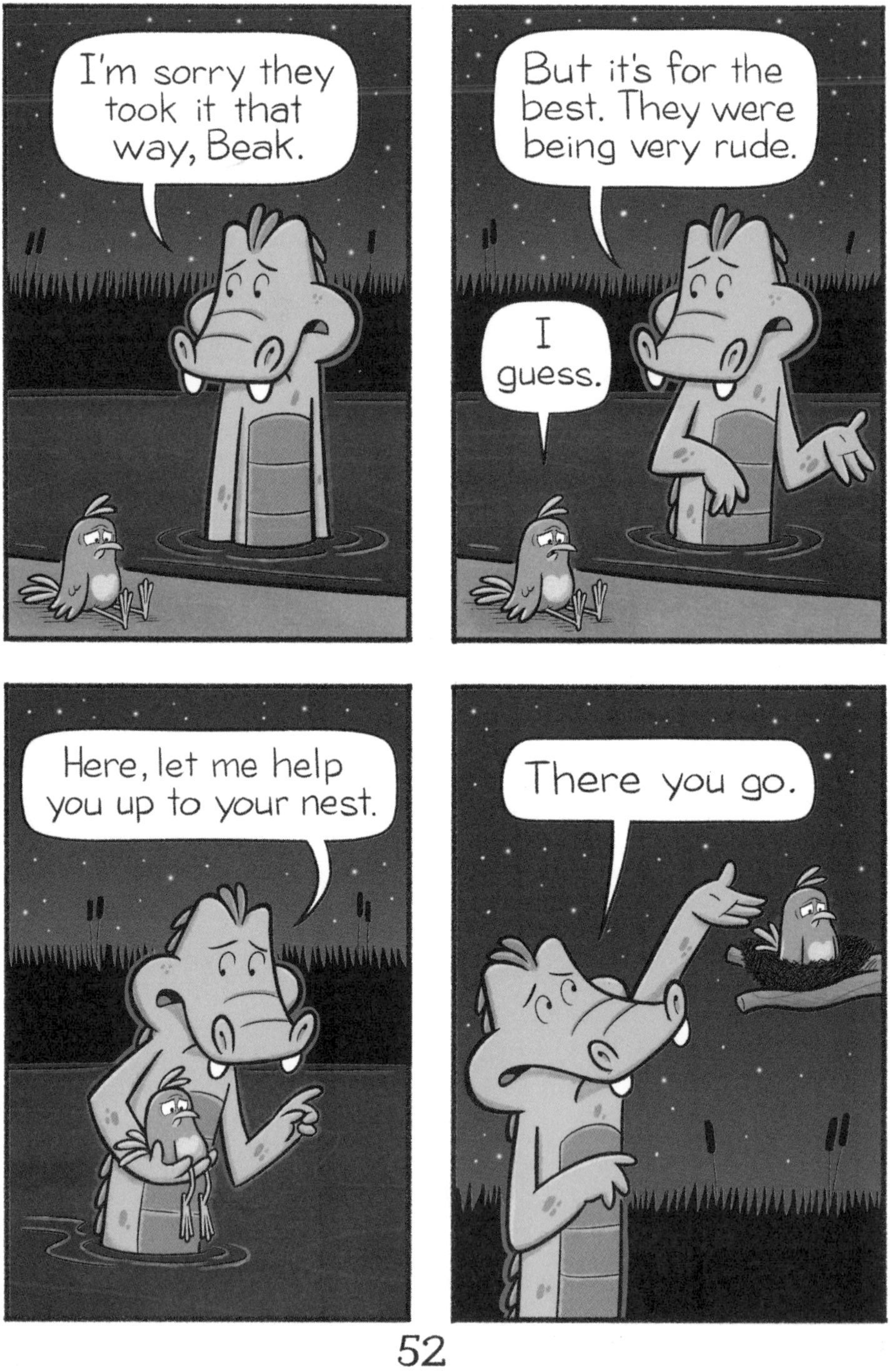
I'm sorry they took it that way, Beak.
But it's for the best. They were being very rude.
I guess.
Here, let me help you up to your nest.
There you go.

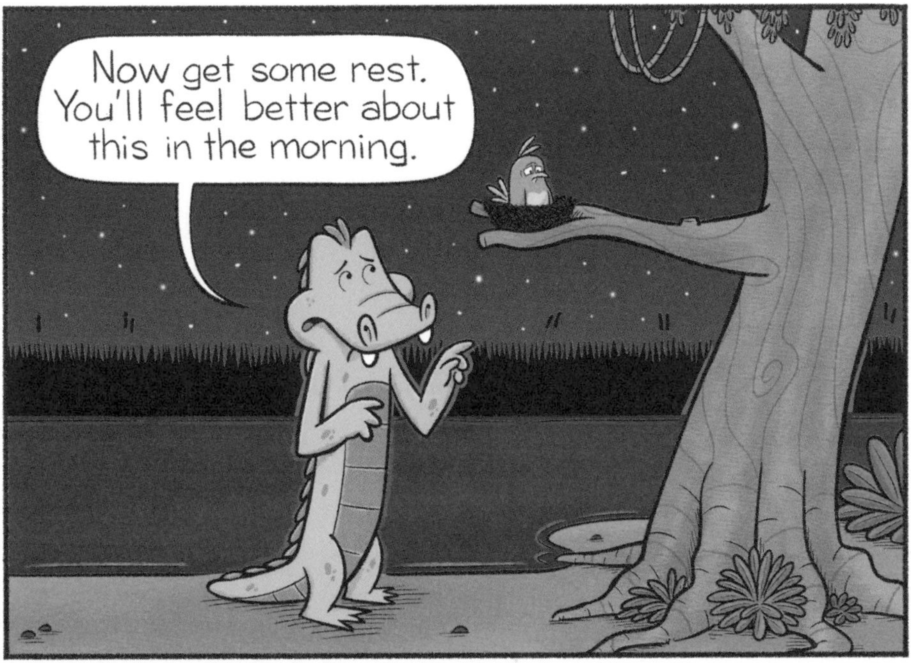
Now get some rest. You'll feel better about this in the morning.

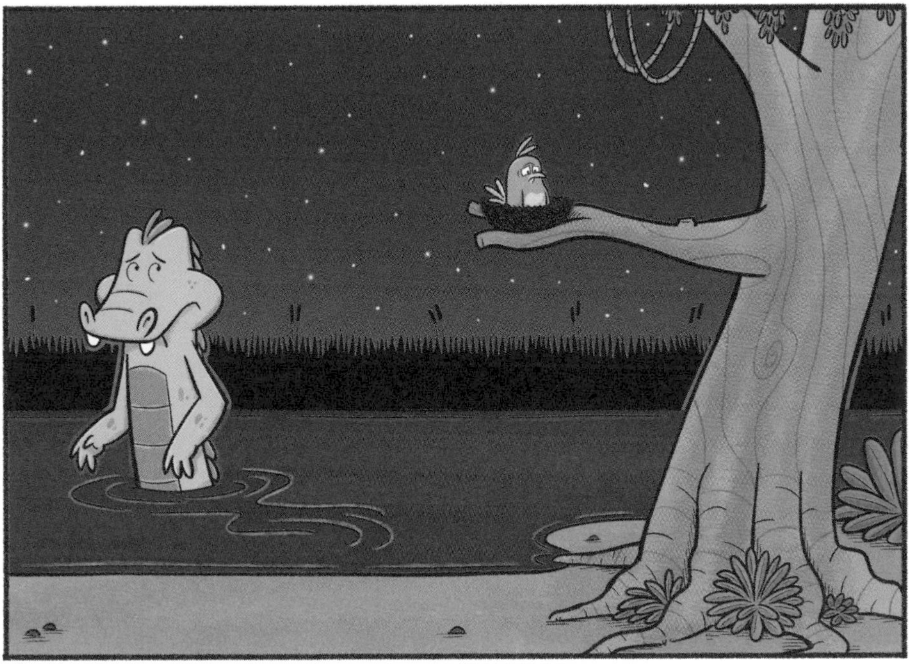

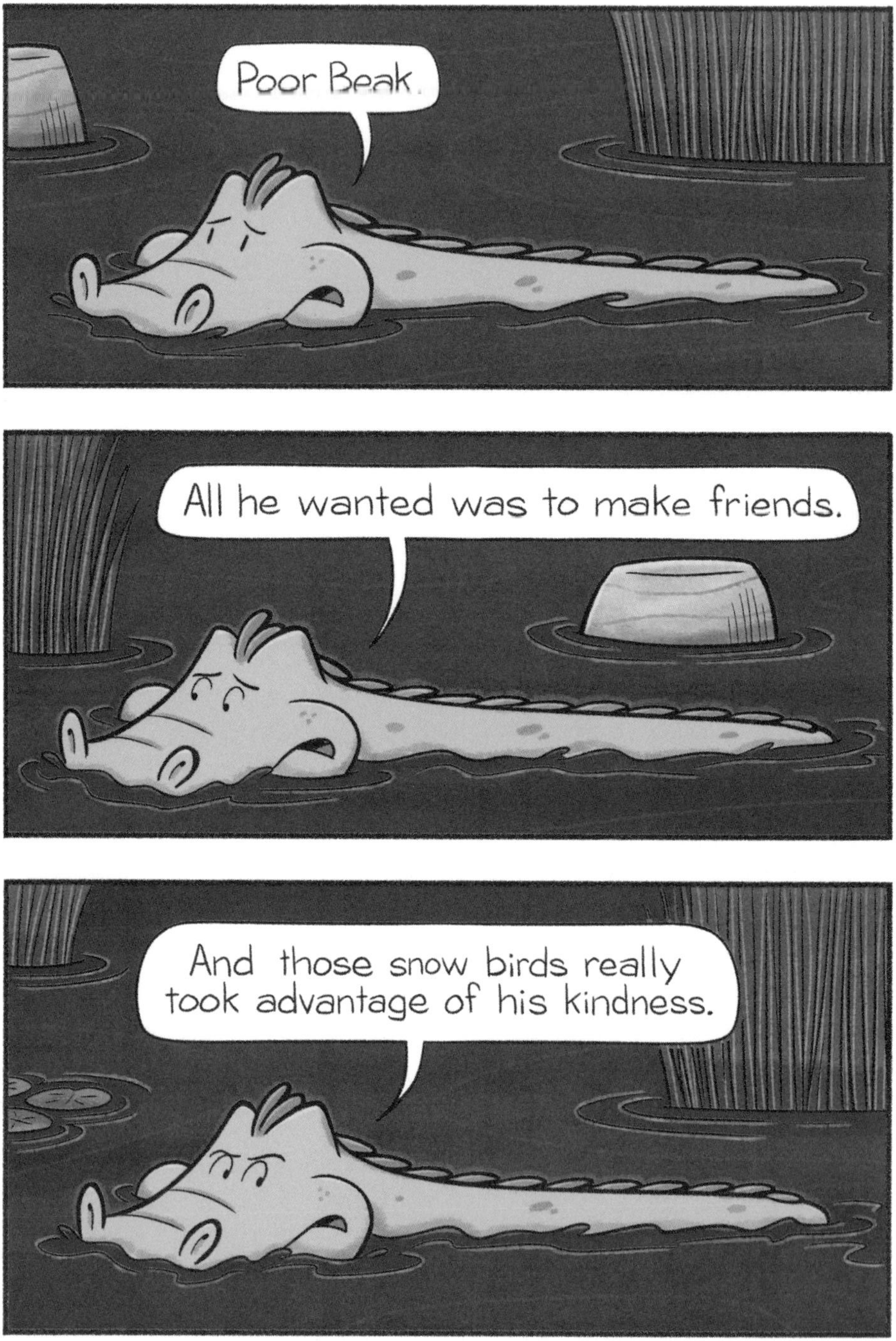
Poor Beak.
All he wanted was to make friends.
And those snow birds really took advantage of his kindness.

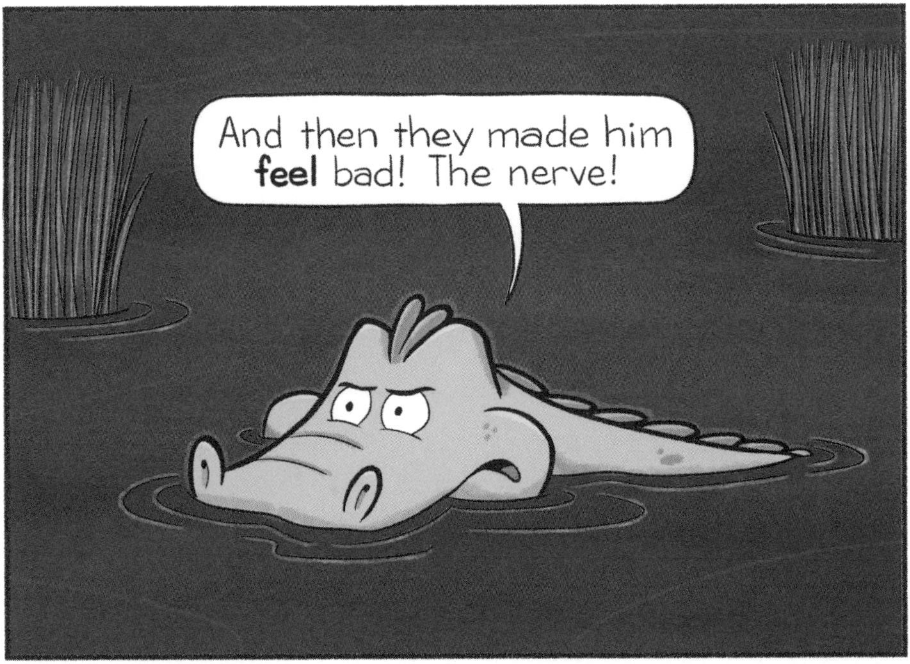
And then they made him **feel** bad! The nerve!

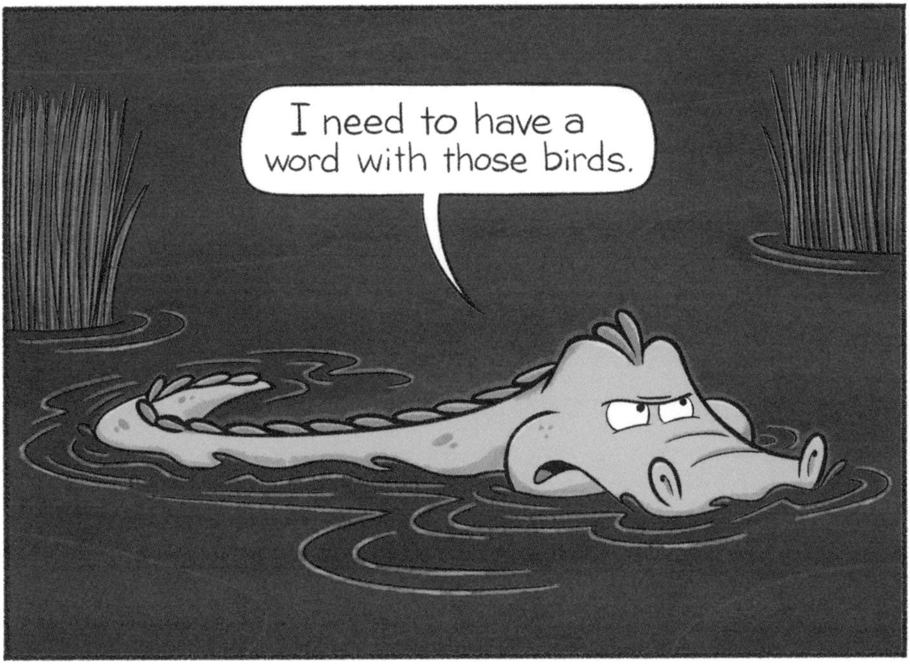
I need to have a word with those birds.

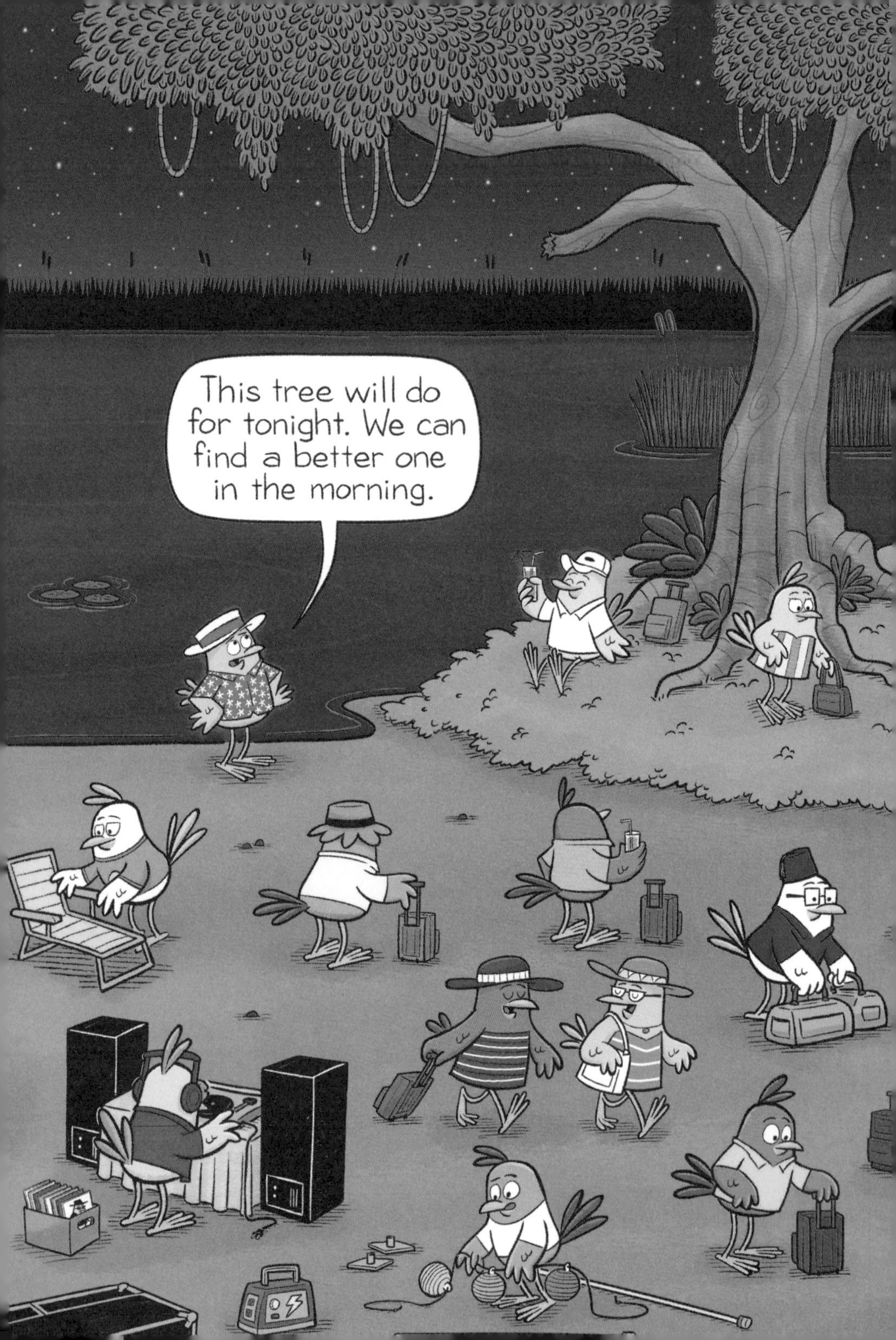
This tree will do for tonight. We can find a better one in the morning.

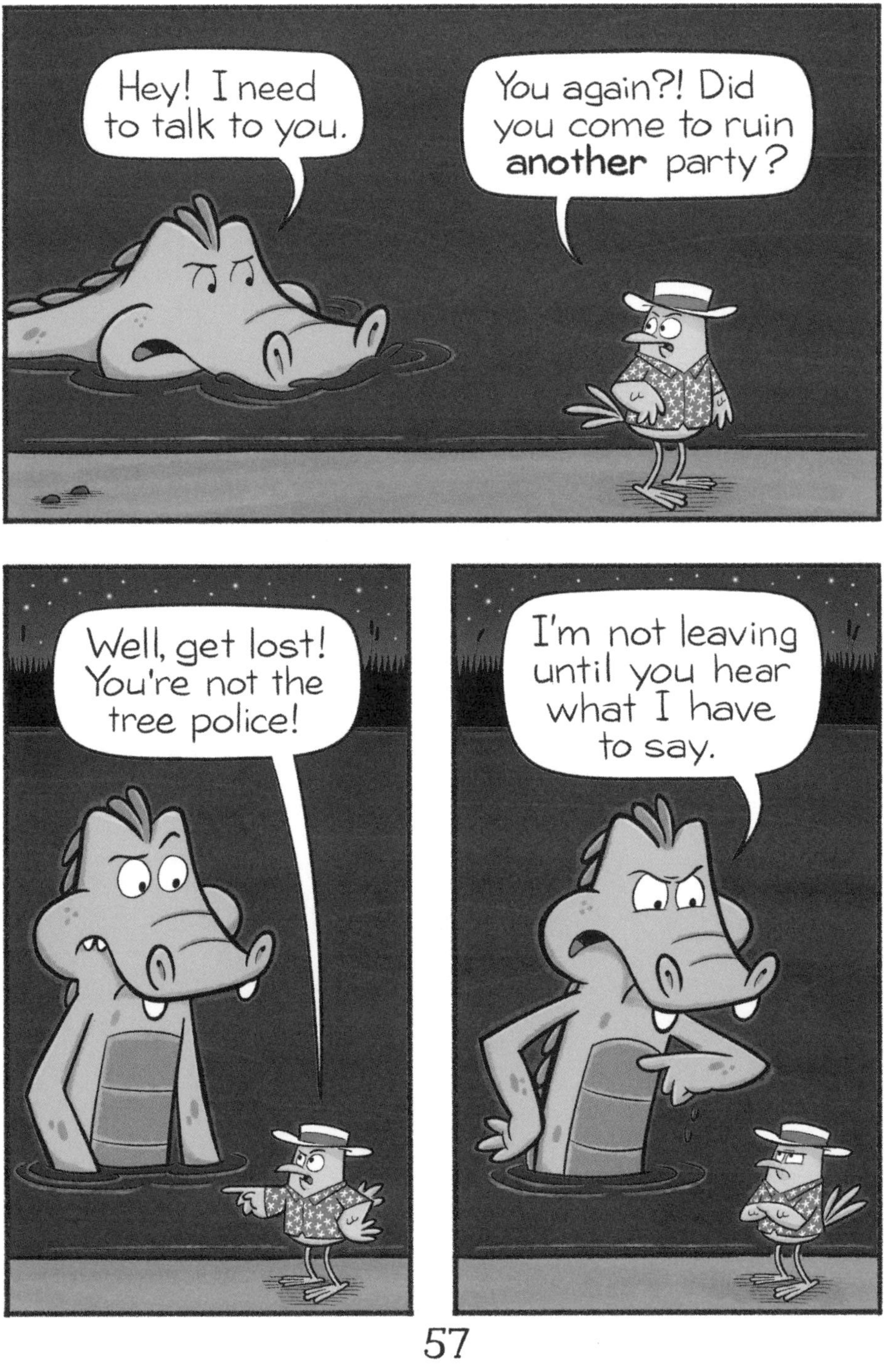
Hey! I need to talk to you.
You again?! Did you come to ruin **another** party?
Well, get lost! You're not the tree police!
I'm not leaving until you hear what I have to say.

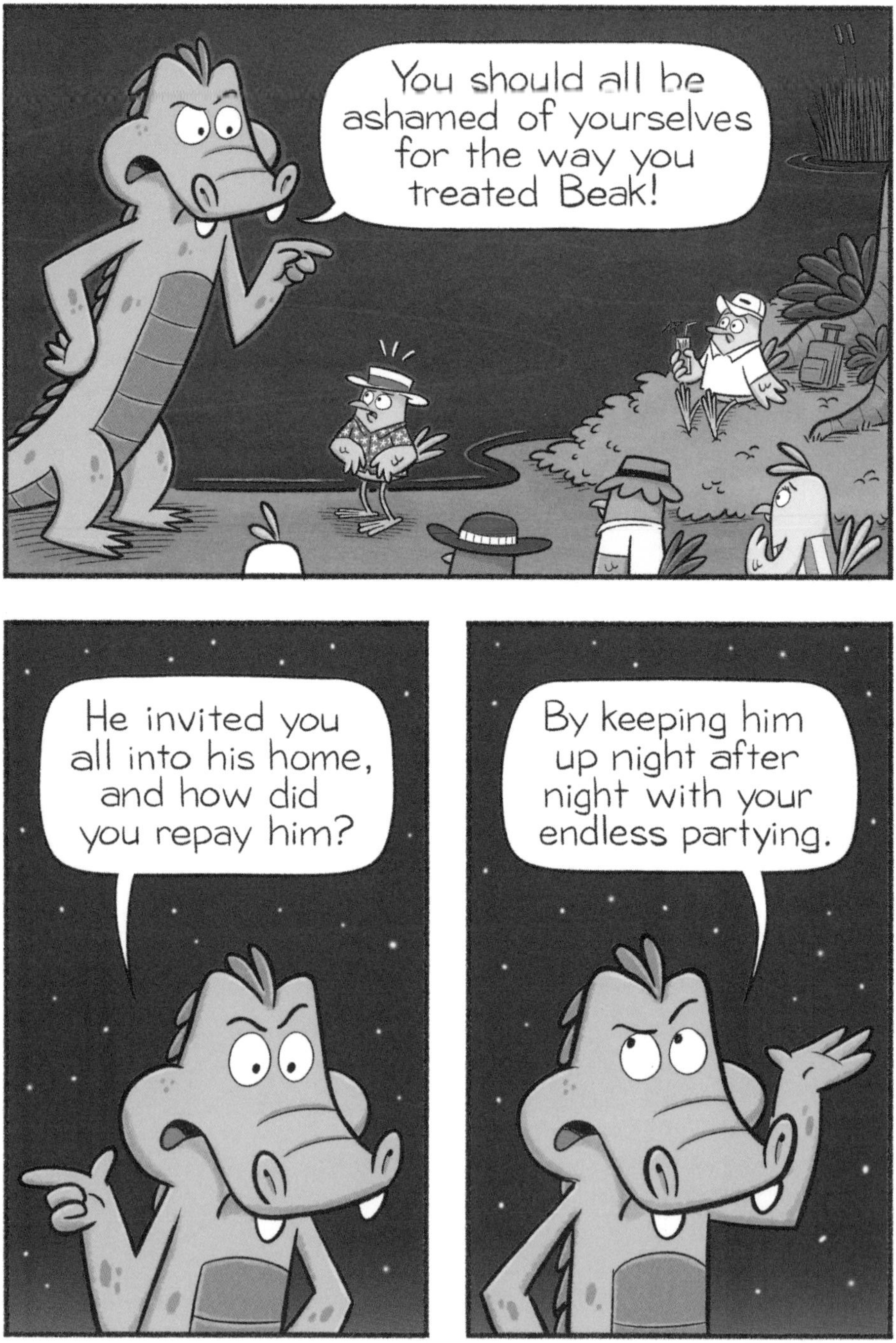
You should all be ashamed of yourselves for the way you treated Beak!
He invited you all into his home, and how did you repay him?
By keeping him up night after night with your endless partying.

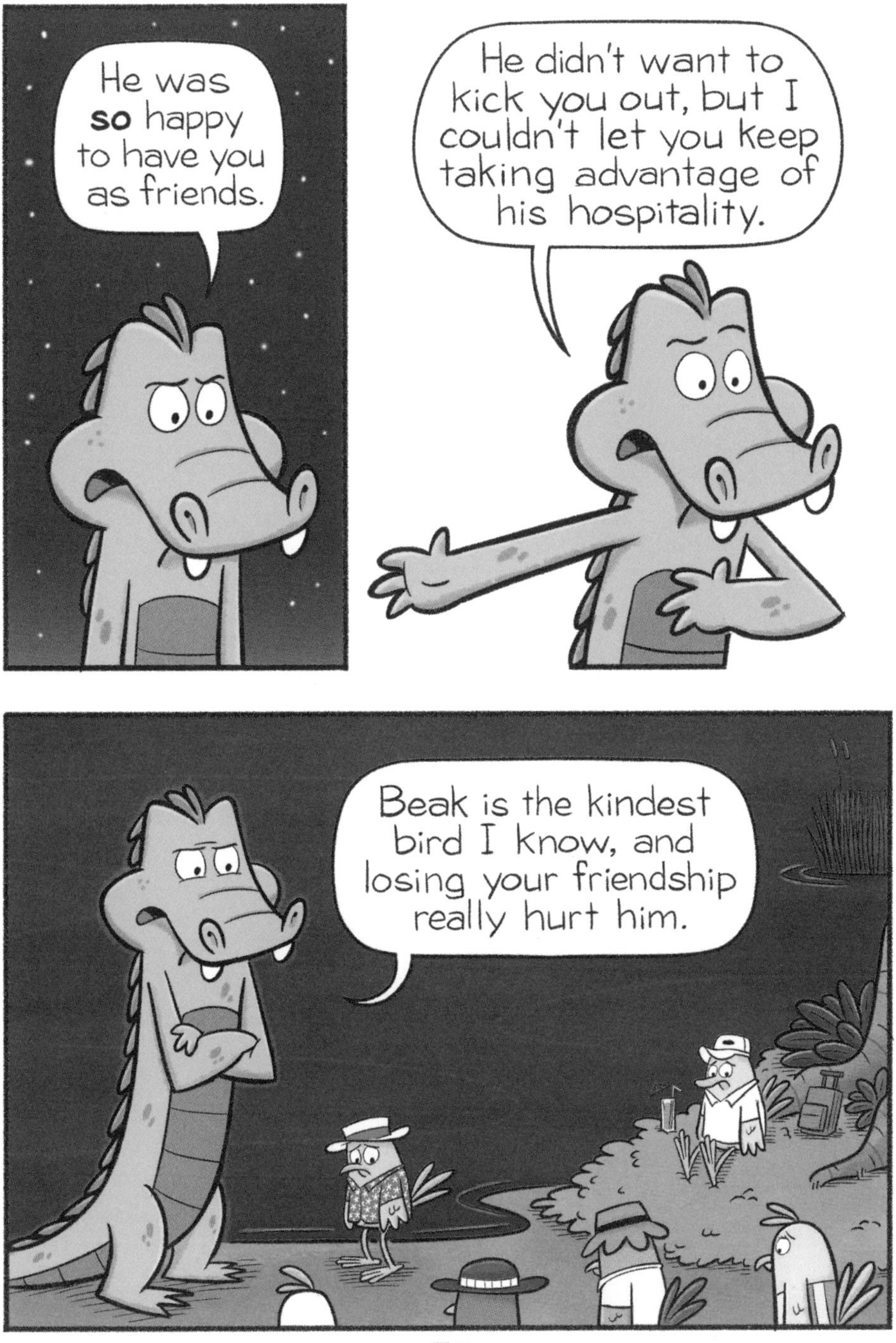
He was **so** happy to have you as friends.
He didn't want to kick you out, but I couldn't let you keep taking advantage of his hospitality.
Beak is the kindest bird I know, and losing your friendship really hurt him.

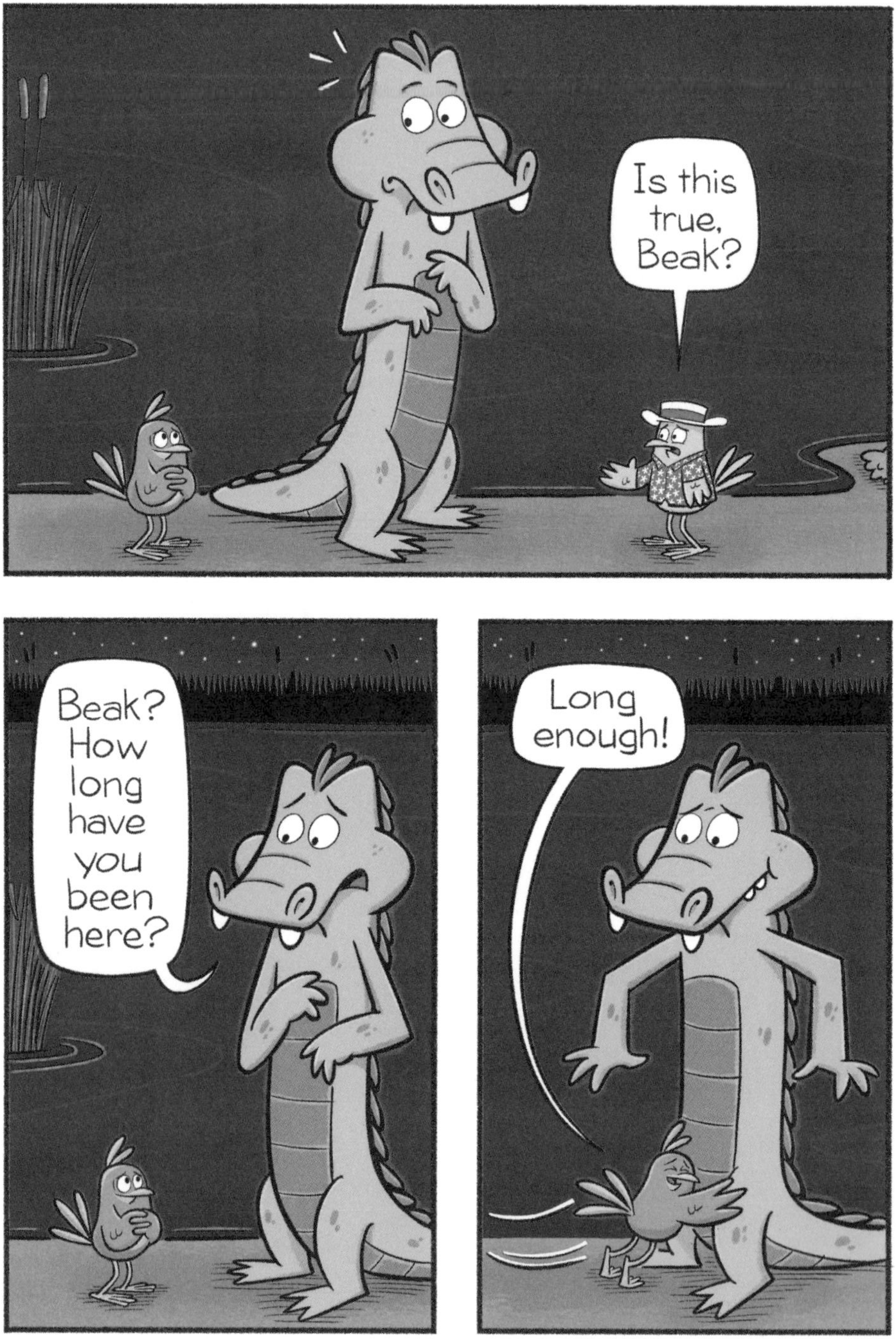
Is this true, Beak?
Beak? How long have you been here?
Long enough!

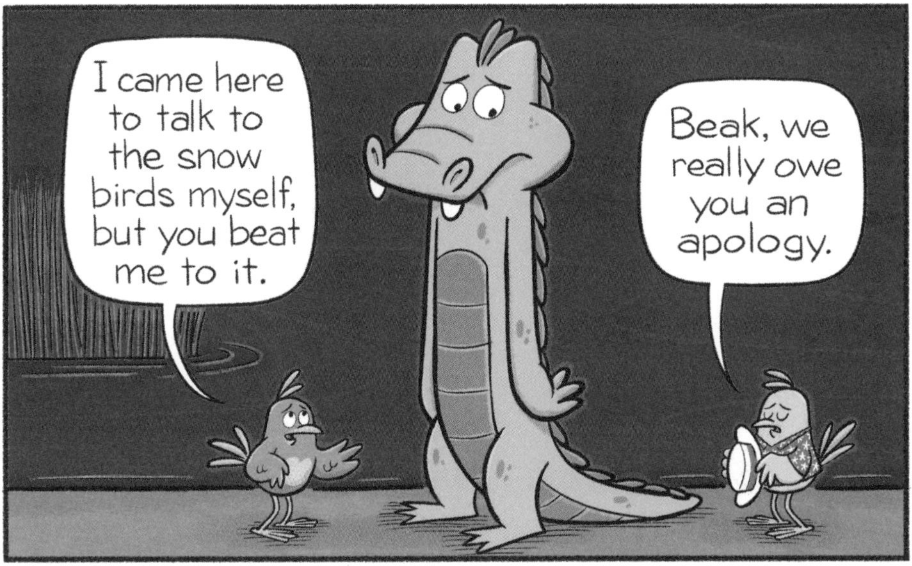
I came here to talk to the snow birds myself, but you beat me to it.
Beak, we really owe you an apology.

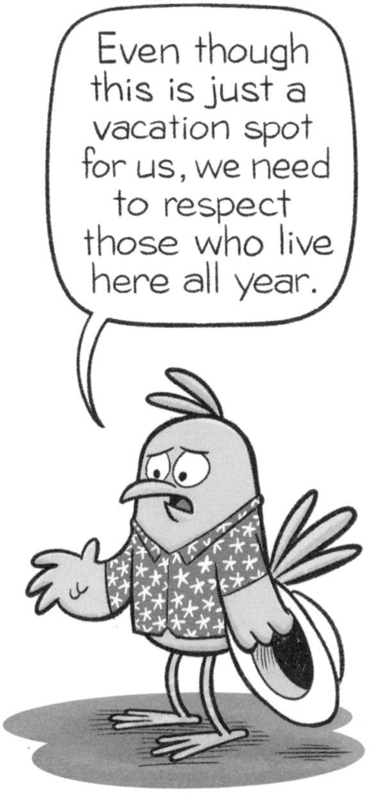
Even though this is just a vacation spot for us, we need to respect those who live here all year.

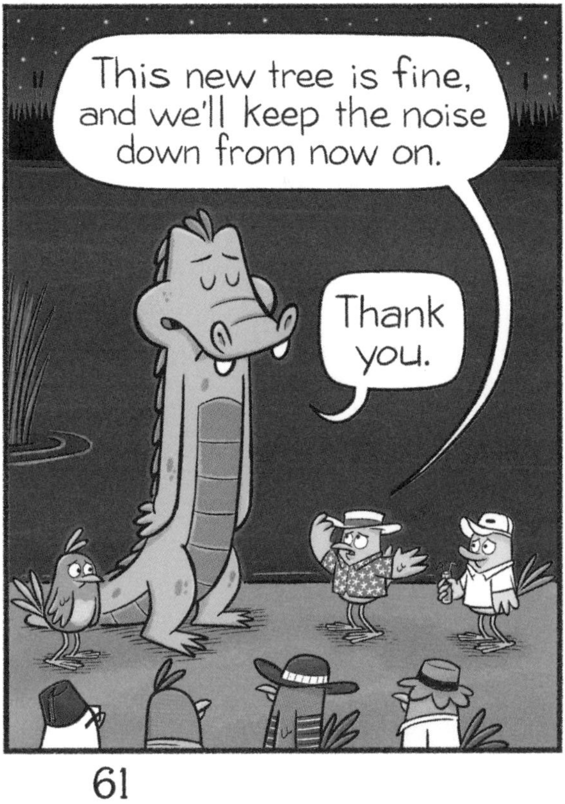
This new tree is fine, and we'll keep the noise down from now on.
Thank you.

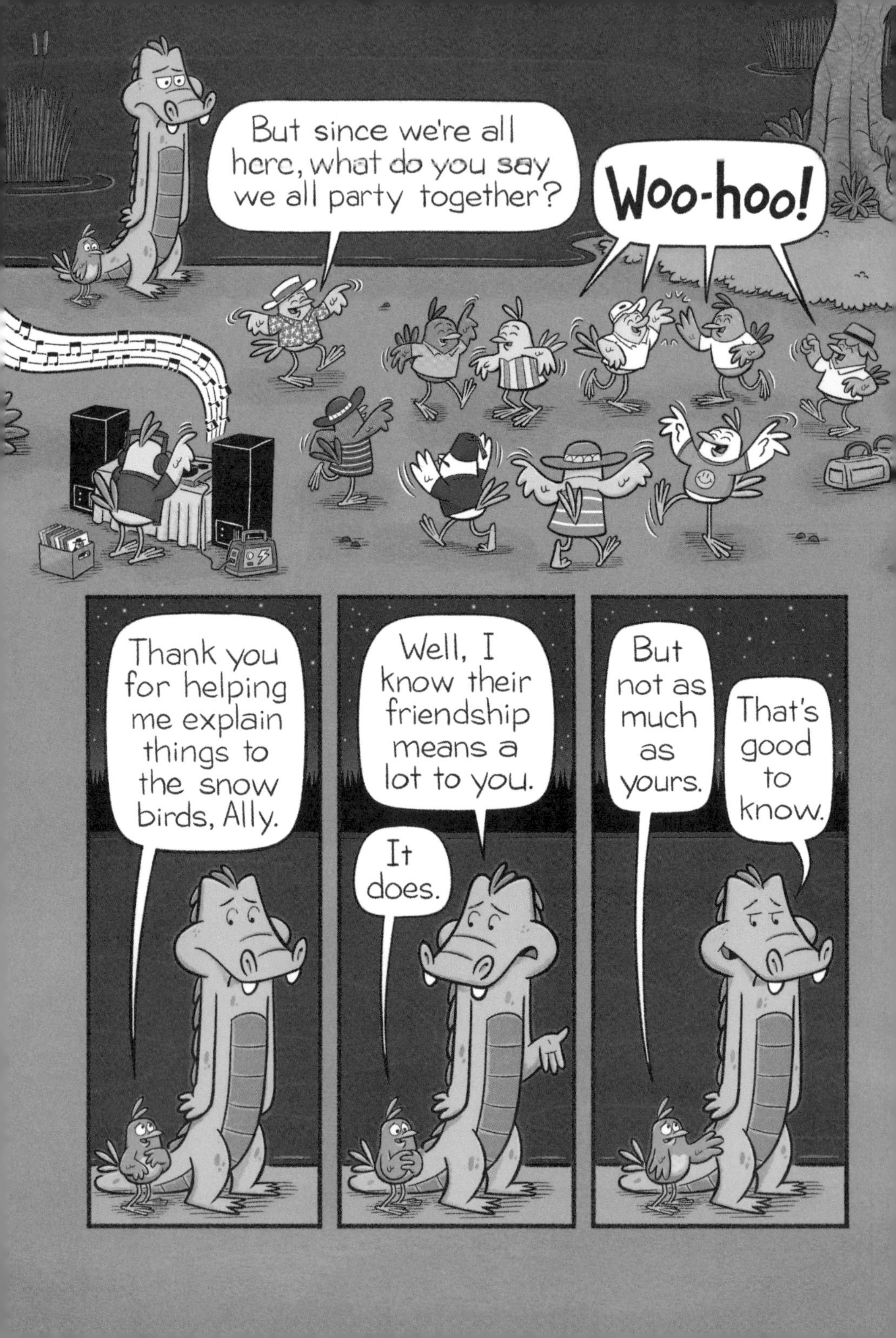
But since we're all here, what do you say we all party together?
Woo-hoo!
Thank you for helping me explain things to the snow birds, Ally.
Well, I know their friendship means a lot to you.
It does.
But not as much as yours.
That's good to know.

HarperAlley is an imprint of HarperCollins Publishers.

Beak & Ally #4: Snow Birds
Copyright © 2023 by Norm Feuti
All rights reserved. Manufactured in Bosnia and Herzegovina.
No part of this book may be used or reproduced in any manner whatsoever without
written permission except in the case of brief quotations embodied in critical articles
and reviews. For information address HarperCollins Children's Books, a division of
HarperCollins Publishers, 195 Broadway, New York, NY 10007.
www.harperalley.com

Library of Congress Control Number: 2022938170
ISBN 978-0-06-302167-9

Typography by Norm Feuti
22 23 24 25 26   GPS   10 9 8 7 6 5 4 3 2 1
First Edition